Shifter High

SH

BUNNY TROUBLE

Season 1, Episodes 2 & 3

Written By

A.J. CULEY

Illustrated By

JEANINE HENNING

Cover art and illustrations by Jeanine Henning

Hardback Edition

ISBN: 978-1-7323286-7-9

Edited by J.L. Troughton

A POOF! Press Publication

For my nephew, Calvin,
who demanded these installments
be written immediately.

The Trouble With THIEVES (a.k.a. Those Blasted Bunnies)

Shifter High: Season 1, Episode 2

Written By

A.J. CULEY

CONTENTS

one

compulsion

IT WAS A compulsion, one Paulie could not ignore. It was the compulsion that had him out here in the woods on a Saturday morning, kneeling in the dirt, digging a hole in the ground. It was the nature of the porcupine-squirrel in him. More porcupine than squirrel physically, more squirrel than porcupine emotionally, it was that squirrelly emotional nature that had Paulie Porcupine digging yet another hole.

He'd tried season after season to ignore the compulsion to dig and he'd failed each time.

Now, having added another failure to his long list of them, Paulie knelt, digging in the dirt, muttering to himself. "Dig-dig-dig-dig-DIG-dig, dig-dig-dig, dig-dig-dig-DIG, dig-dig-diiiig-dig, dig-dig, dig-dig-dig-dig, DIG!"

What was that?

Paulie looked around furtively and saw nothing. He spun around in a circle, moving swiftly on his knees, head jerking in frantic movements, trying to see what he'd heard. There was nothing around him. He listened, but heard nothing. He was all alone, no one to witness his digging. After a moment, Paulie crouched back over his hole and began frantically digging again. "Dig-dig-dig-dig-dig-dig-dig, dig-dig-dig-dig-dig-dig, dig-DIG-dig-dig, dig-dig-dig-dig, dig-dig-DIG-di—"

"What are you doing?"

Paulie scrambled back and looked up.

Worst thing ever.

It was that girl.

Amelia.

She was in his art and technology classes and she was really smart … and really human.

"What are you doing?" she asked again.

"Nothing!" Paulie said. "Nothing, nothing to see, nothing-nothing-nothing!" He knelt back over his hole and began to dig again. "Dig-dig-dig-dig, dig-DIG, dig-dig-dig, dig-diiiig-dig-DIG!"

"It is too something. You're digging," said the girl.

Amelia.

Amelia, the human girl.

The human girl who needed to go away.

"Go-go-go. Dig-dig-dig-go." Why wouldn't she go away? "Dig-dig-dig-go."

"Why are you digging?"

"No reason, nothing-nothing to see." Go away-way-way! "Dig-dig-dig-go, dig-dig-DIG."

The human girl crouched in front of him, the hole he was digging between them. "I'm Amelia."

He already knew her name. Knew who she was. Knew she was

human. A human who needed to go away.

"What's your name?"

"Paulie-Paulie, my name's Paulie." Go away-way-way.

"It's nice to meet you, Paulie. Why are you digging?"

Why was she so curious? Couldn't she see he was busy? "No reason. Dig-dig-dig." Though Paulie tried to make his hands stop digging, the more agitated he became, the faster his hands moved, digging and digging and digging. He just couldn't stop himself. Like he'd said, it was a compulsion, something he couldn't avoid, couldn't resist. He had to dig. It was the squirrel in him, the damn squirrel!

"So, what are you going to put in the hole once it's dug?"

"Nothing, nothing-nothing-nothing!" Paulie's hands slowed and he peered into the hole. It was't very wide. Wide enough though. But was it deep enough? He pawed at the dirt a bit. It was. Just deep enough. It was a perfectly sized hole.

"So what's down there?"

"Nothing, nothing!" Paulie flung his body over the hole, to keep her from seeing what was inside it. Still crouched there, he looked all around them. Was anyone watching, anyone besides the human girl? Had anyone seen him digging this hole?

Were there bunnies around?

Those darn bunnies.

But he saw nothing.

"Come on, let me see," said the human girl. "I can help."

"No-no-no!" She couldn't help. She wasn't a squirrel! Besides, this was his job. His job to dig.

And because he just couldn't help himself, Paulie sat up and began to dig some more. "Dig-dig-dig, diiiig deep-deep-deep, dig-dig deep."

There!

It was the perfect amount of depth, perfectly even on all sides, a perfectly formed hole.

He looked at the human girl, then reached behind him as if he had something there, grabbed a handful and shoved it down deep into the hole and started to cover it, fast.

"What was that?"

"Nothing, nothing, nothing at all!" Paulie continued patting dirt down over his hidden prize.

"Come on!" The human girl nudged Paulie aside so she could see into the hole. "There's nothing there. Did you already cover it?" Reaching down, she began to dig, pushing away the dirt Paulie had just used to cover what he'd hidden. "There really isn't anything here."

Paulie gasped and looked around. Had anyone heard what she'd just said? Was anyone watching, listening?

He didn't see anyone.

Except the human girl. She was looking at Paulie as if he were crazy. He wasn't crazy! Why did people always look at him like that?

"Why are you digging a hole for nothing?"

"Not nothing!" Paulie scowled and began to fill in his hole. "Fill-fill, cover-cover, hide it away-way-way."

"But there's nothing there." She stared into the hole.

Why did she keep saying that? It wasn't nothing. It wasn't. And now he would have to find another place to bury his not-nothing, just because she knew where he'd buried this not-nothing. Paulie's hands moved faster and faster, shoving dirt back into the hole as fast as he could, all the while chanting, "bury-bury-bury-bury-bury-bury-bury-bury-bury-bury."

"I don't understand."

Well, why would she? Paulie ignored her and continued filling in his hole, faster and faster. "Bury-bury-bury-bury." The human girl couldn't possibly understand. After all, she had no squirrel in her, no animal at all really, she was kind of boring that way. Still– "Here!" he snapped at her as he continued moving dirt, filling in his hole. "Bury-bury-bury."

Finally, it was done. He patted the ground until it was nice and smooth, then pulled a few leaves and bits of grass over to lay on top of his buried treasure, strategically hiding the view of recently dug dirt.

He tilted his head and stared at the spot. Maybe it was a little too well-hidden. Reaching out, he knocked a few leaves this way and that, moving the foliage just enough, just enough, there. Now some of the freshly-hidden dirt was revealed in one small area, just enough to maybe entice some rotten, thievin' varmint.

"Good, looks good, looks good-good-good."

"Looks kind of the same to me."

Paulie jumped.

He'd forgotten she was there.

That human girl.

Still here.

Still watching.

Was she going to tell anyone about this?

He'd have to move his treasure.

But not today.

Later when she wasn't around. Find a better hiding spot.

"Are you done digging now?"

"No. Maybe. No." Was he? Paulie thought for a minute. The compulsion seemed to have passed. Maybe he was done. Yes. Yes, he felt good, peaceful.

The compulsion was gone.

The hole had been dug, the treasure buried, the spot hidden.

Even though a human had seen his spot, he was pretty sure she wouldn't be interested in his treasure, any of his treasures. So that was okay.

As long as she didn't tell the bunnies. He eyed her. She did eat with the bunnies at lunch the other day. Didn't she know the bunnies couldn't be trusted? Those blasted bunnies.

Paulie stood and smacked his hands against his knees, dislodging dirt from both.

The human girl stood as well.

Amelia. She was tall.

For a human.

Well, taller than him anyway, but then Paulie was short. It was the squirrel in him! And the porcupine. Got it from both sides.

Still. Didn't seem right that a human would be taller than a shifter of any kind.

"So, Paulie. We're in a couple classes together, right? Art and technology?"

"Art, yes. Peaceful. Calm. And technology. Computers. Easy to understand."

"Right. Much easier than people."

Especially human people. "Yes-yes."

"Anyway, I wanted to thank you for saving me from Mr. Fox my first day in tech."

Paulie shrugged. Mr. Fox hadn't exactly been thrilled to find out a human would be in his class. Paulie could understand completely.

Humans were so annoying.

"So, what are you gonna do now? What does everyone do on the weekends around here?"

Paulie had no idea what to say. There really was nothing they did for fun that would be safe for a human girl to participate in. Where could he send her where no one would be shifted? "There's bowling."

"Yes. So I've heard. Every time I go to the bowling alley, though, it's empty. No one's ever there. I don't even know why it's open."

It was open because the town council had researched humans and had decided a bowling alley and movie theater were their best options for human entertainment. "Movies! There's a theater downtown."

"That only shows one movie. I've already seen it."

That was a problem? Paulie would have to tell the council so they could switch movies.

"And that movie's been out a decade."

What did that mean? It was a problem if the movie had been out for a while? Humans were so complicated. Demanding. Needy.

"What else do you do besides bowl or go to the only movie in town?"

"Nothing. I just stay at home. Watch my little brothers and sisters. Most of us do that. We don't really have any fun around here. Maybe you and your dad should move." Paulie didn't really want her to move.

He thought it was kind of funny, watching the grown-ups run around town, trying to keep the humans from discovering their secret. He figured it was just a matter of time. Eventually the humans would figure things out and then the fun would really start.

He wasn't going to be the one to tell them though. He'd just let them discover it on their own.

In the meantime, he'd go along with the town's plans.

"Why do people keep saying that to me?"

Paulie jumped. Saying what? What had he said?

"The town invited my dad here. They needed a vet! Now it's like no one wants us around. My dad's not going to agree to move just because the town's changed its mind. They're gonna have to fire him!"

Well, that was an idea. If things didn't work out, maybe the town would fire the man and then things could get back to normal. As normal as they ever were in Shifterville.

"I mean, I've never been anywhere so less welcoming of its new residents," Amelia ranted, "and I've lived in cities all over this country. This place is crazy. We're not moving!"

"Well." Paulie shrugged. "Guess you're just gonna have to be bored, bored, bored then. I've gotta get back to — you know — counting, counting, counting—"

Don't say acorns, don't say acorns, don't say acorns.

"—um—"

"Yes?"

"Nothing. Um. Nothing. Just counting, just counting. See you later, later. At school. Next week. Yeah. Bye." Paulie turned away and started counting as he strode through the woods. "One, two, three-four-five, six, seven, eight, nine, ten-eleven, twelve, thirteen, fourteen, fifteen, sixteen, seventeen-eighteen, nineteen."

Amelia stared as Paulie disappeared into the woods, his voice fading as he walked further away. She had no idea what he was counting. Steps maybe? Leaves on the ground? She wondered how high he would count and if he would start his count over tomorrow or keep counting up as far as he could go.

He was an interesting guy.

Different, which was always a plus in her mind.

She shouldn't have given him a hard time about burying nothing. There was probably a perfectly logical explanation. Maybe not to her, but whatever he'd been doing, she was sure it made perfect sense to him.

She stared at the ground, where Paulie had been digging. She kind of wanted to dig it back up, just to check and see. Had he really been burying nothing? Or was there something there, something he'd buried before she'd arrived?

two

bunnies

"WAIT A MINUTE, wait a minute. Let me get this straight." Melvin couldn't believe what he was hearing. "You—"

"Yeah, yeah, yeah."

"Wow."

"Yeah, I know, I know, I know."

"So she caught you burying—"

"Yes, yes, she did."

"Your winter stores."

"Yes, okay, yes! She did."

"Wow, I don't even know what to say to that, Paulie. I mean no one in this town has caught you burying your stores. And now, of all people, Amelia's the one who catches you? By now, she definitely thinks we're all crazy, which I guess we really are, because you know, not exactly average over here in Shifterville."

"That's true, true, true. But you know, it's not as bad as it sounds."

"How's that?"

"Well, technically, she caught me burying my fake winter stores."

"Your fake winter stores."

"Yeah, you know. The ones I bury to fool the bunny-bunnies. So the location of my real winter stores hasn't been compromised. Thank goodness."

"Right. Because that's what I was worried about."

"Well, you should be! Those bunny-bunnies will have me starving, Melvin, if they get even half a chance!"

"Please, you're not in danger of starving, Paulie."

"Why does everyone always say that, say that? I'm not in danger only because I bury my winter stores."

"Your false winter stores."

"Sure, but I bury both. I mean, you know, I bury the real thing all quiet-quiet, where no one can find them, and I bury my false stores, still quiet, but maybe just a little not-quiet, to fool the bunny-bunnies, you see."

"What are you going on about now?"

"The bunnies, man, the bunnies! Those thievin', blasted bunnies. They're always stealing my winter stores."

"Well, you're burying them outside, Paulie. It's bound to happen. You're a shifter, you live in a house. Put 'em in your pantry, for heaven's sake."

"Why would I do that? Everyone knows that's where food is stored. Anyone could find it, find it there! I keep telling my parents that, but do they listen to me? No, no, no! And my mom's a squirrel. I mean, really, 100% squirrel-squirrel, and she just doesn't get it. Why doesn't anyone understand what I'm saying? Those bunny-bunnies can burrow anywhere. They can get into our house, find our winter stores in the pantry where everyone stores them, and then where will we be? In Starvation City, that's where! In the County of Cannibalism! I don't want to become a cannibal, Melvin! You should hide your food too. Everyone should hide their food!"

"Okay, calm down, Mr. Nutters. Everything's going to be just fine."

Paulie huffed. "Why does everyone keep calling me that, as if it's a bad thing? I'm a squirrel! Of course, I'm a little nutter-nutters."

"Porcupine. Let's be clear. You're a porcupine."

"Porcupine-squirrel!"

"Right."

three

the missing acorns

"MELVIN, WAIT UP, up, up!" Paulie darted in and out of the students in the hallway, trying to catch up to Melvin, whose long legs carried him everywhere too fast, too fast.

Melvin paused outside his history class and Paulie latched onto his arm. "Come on, let's go-go-go."

"Go where? I've got history and aren't you supposed to be in art?"

"This is too important. I gotta talk, talk, talk to you."

"But the bell's gonna ring."

Paulie pulled on Melvin's arm. "Come on. Melvin, this is important-portant. Please!" The moose was just too big to move, but Paulie refused to give up. He kept tugging and tugging.

Melvin sighed. "Fine. Where are we going?"

"This way, come on!" Paulie dragged him down the hall, a feat that was much easier now that Melvin was finally cooperating. They reached the supply closet just as the bell rang. Paulie paused, glanced around, then jerked open the door and darted inside with Melvin on his heels.

The door closed behind them.

"For shift's sake, it's dark in here," Melvin muttered.

"It's not that dark," Paulie said.

"For you maybe. Moose aren't nocturnal, you know."

"Whatever. Melvin, you've gotta help me!"

"Why? What's wrong?"

"That girl, Amelia. She told the bunny-bunnies. I know she did!"

"Told them what?"

"About my acorn-acorns. Now they're gone, not just the fake ones, but the real ones too. Someone stole my acorns, Melvin, and I bet it was that Amelia and her blasted, thievin' bunny-bunny friends!"

"Why would you think that, Paulie?"

"Because she saw me, didn't she? She saw me in the woods, dig-digging that hole, bury-burying my fake winter stores. She's probably been following me all along, watching where I bury my acorns, telling the bunny-bunnies, helping them steal from me."

"I thought you liked Amelia."

"Well that was before I knew she wanted me to starve!"

"I seriously doubt that. Amelia doesn't seem the type to care about your acorns. Besides, humans don't eat acorns. I don't think."

"But the bunny-bunnies do! And she's assigned to their cafeteria so she probably gave them my acorn-acorns."

"Why would she do that, Paulie?"

"I don't know. Probably because they're friends."

"Paulie."

"Fine. You don't have to believe me, just help-help-help me."

"Help you what?"

"Get my acorn-acorns back."

"I thought you said she gave them to the bunnies."

"Well, I don't know that, do I? Maybe she bury-buried them in a new spot."

"I don't think–"

"Don't think. Just help-help!"

"Fine. What do you want us to do?"

"Follow her."

"Follow Amelia?"

"Yes, yes, we need to follow her. See what she's up-up-up to, see what she's doing with my acorn-acorns, who she's stealing them for."

Melvin sighed. "All right. When?"

"This afternoon."

"Fine. I'll meet you in the courtyard after classes. You know it's gonna be kind of difficult to keep her from seeing us."

"We'll be subtle. She won't even notice us, especially if we shift."

"Are you crazy? A porcupine and a moose lumbering after a human? And you don't think she'll notice?"

Paulie hesitated. That was a good point. Moose weren't exactly known for their stealth abilities. "Fine. You can stay human. I'll go spiny."

"I can't go near Amelia. You know what happens when I get too close."

"I thought we'd solved that issue!"

"Not when I have to dress out in P.E. every afternoon. Mr. Grizzly was furious when I came out in human form last week. He made me do a thousand push-ups while everyone else played clawball."

"That's quilled up. You missed out on claw-clawball?"

"Yes, I did. It sucked moose balls."

"So you're back to avoiding Amelia, is that it?"

"Yes, yes I am."

"Okay, we'll just stay way back when we're following her."

"Great. We need to get to class. I'll see you after school. We'll figure everything out then, okay?"

"Quillerific!"

four

the moose

AMELIA WAS WORKING on a sketch of the moose she'd seen walking on the side of the road the week before when the art room door burst open and Paulie appeared, looking frazzled.

"Paulie Porcupine."

Amelia really liked Mrs. Spider, but her voice, so soft and menacing, made the hair on the back of Amelia's neck stand straight up. It felt as if all the air had been sucked out of the room as Paulie froze in the doorway and stared at Mrs. Spider with wide eyes.

"Sorry-sorry-sorry, Mrs. Spider-Spider. Had a terrible-terrible bathroom emergency."

A couple kids behind Amelia snorted, but she couldn't drag her eyes away from the picture Paulie made in the doorway. He was about half the size of Mrs. Spider and was clinging to the doorknob, a look of terror on his face.

Mrs. Spider loomed over him, her tall, thin form contrasting sharply against Paulie's much shorter frame. "Fine," she snapped. "Get to work now, young man."

Paulie edged passed Mrs. Spider, then headed for Amelia, an unhappy look on his face.

Amelia wondered if it was because the only empty space was right next to her. He hadn't seemed to mind sitting by her last week, but this week he'd been different. Thank goodness for Felicia, who was sitting on her other side, and acted as friendly as always.

All the other kids ignored her, except for when she walked by their work area. Then they would quickly cover their art, as if afraid she would steal their ideas or something. Like she couldn't come up with unique artwork on her own. She was fine with it though. As far as she was concerned, ignoring her and hiding their artwork was way better than the kid in calculus who was constantly staring and sniffing at her hair, generally freaking her out.

Paulie plopped into the chair beside her, then immediately began to edge it away from her. She wasn't sure what his problem was. He'd been mostly normal last week, even friendly on occasion. This week not so much. Sure he hadn't exactly been thrilled to see her in the woods over the weekend, but he hadn't ignored her either.

"Hi, Paulie," Amelia said, just to see if he'd acknowledge her.

"Amelia," he squeaked.

"How's it going? Been out in the woods lately?"

Paulie's eyes bugged out.

Okay, that was kind of mean. "I'm just kidding, Paulie. Really. Just giving you a hard time."

He stared at her suspiciously, then edged his chair even further away. He grabbed his easel and dragged it over so it was in front of him, then angled it so she couldn't see his blank canvas.

Amelia sighed. This was getting old.

She turned her attention back to the moose she was drawing. She was having trouble with the antlers, getting their size just right. She erased the antler on the left and sketched it again. Bigger. That was better. Glancing around, she saw that no one was watching, so she quickly sketched in a bookbag hanging from it. She closed her eyes and tried to picture the bookbag again. There'd been an ornament of some kind hanging from the strap, but she couldn't remember it exactly.

"Hey, that looks like–"

Amelia opened her eyes.

Paulie was standing next to her, staring at her picture of the moose, eyes wide.

"It looks like what?"

Paulie shook his head. "Nothing-nothing-nothing."

"Hey, that's pretty good, Amelia," Felicia now stood on her other side.

"Yes, but why'd you draw a bookbag on his antler-antler? That is a bookbag, right?"

"Yeah." Amelia grabbed an eraser and started erasing the bag.

"Wait, why are you erasing it?" Felicia asked.

"It's something I learned in my old art class. My teacher said if you're not sure the perspective's right, I mean the size or whatever, you should try drawing an ordinary object next to what you're working on, to see the size difference. You know. Then once you're sure you've got the perspective right, you can erase the object." Well, her teacher had said something like that, but that wasn't why Amelia had drawn the bookbag. She wasn't going to share with Paulie and Felicia that she thought she'd seen an actual moose carrying one though. Paulie was already suspicious enough of her without making him think she was crazy too. And Felicia was pretty much the only one in school who liked her at the moment, so she wasn't going to risk losing that.

"I guess that makes sense." Paulie continued staring at the sketch with a weird look on his face.

Amelia waited, but he didn't say anything else. "What?" She finally demanded.

Paulie jumped. "What-what?"

"Why do you keep staring at my moose? Go work on your own project."

"Sorry-sorry. It's just very lifelike. Looks a lot, a lot like–" he stopped and didn't say anything more, just stared at her canvas.

"Like a real moose, right, Paulie?" Felicia said.

"Right-right, a real moose, right."

Amelia shook her head. She doubted that's what he'd been going to say, but whatever. "Well, that's the point, isn't it?"

"Sure-sure-sure." He turned away.

"You're really good at drawing," Felicia said. "He's right. It's very lifelike."

"Thanks."

Felicia returned to her seat and Amelia went back to contemplating the moose.

The eyes weren't quite right. They should be rounder or something. She worked on them a bit, then went back to the antlers.

Their size was pretty good now, but the one on the left looked naked without the bookbag so she quickly sketched it in again. As absurd as it was, she liked the moose with the bookbag hanging off its antler. He looked friendlier that way. More cartoonish and less wild.

Before she could change her mind, she grabbed her pens and began to ink him in.

five

cafeteria a

AFTER ART, AMELIA had English, then lunch in Cafeteria A where she joined Felicia and Luis again. At least this time, Mrs. Saber had let her walk to the cafeteria on her own. No more lectures about Cafeteria A and how she was only allowed to eat there. Thank goodness. Amelia had so many questions she couldn't wait to ask her friends. Like how many cafeterias there were in all and why she couldn't eat in any of the others.

Felicia and Luis didn't seem to have any answers though.

Luis hemmed and hawed until Felicia finally said, "Well, there are four cafeterias."

Luis gave her a wide-eyed look and she just shrugged.

Amelia couldn't decide which was more perplexing: the fact that there were four cafeterias or the fact that they seemed to be top secret. "So are they all like this one?"

Luis snorted and Felicia giggled.

"Not really," Felicia said. "This one's the vegetarian cafeteria. The others ..." She hesitated. "...aren't."

"So... meat then?"

"Lots of meat," Luis said and Felicia nodded.

"So everyone in here's a vegetarian?"

"Pretty much," Felicia said.

"That's a lot of vegetarians."

"Not enough though." Felicia scowled. "I wish everyone else would stop eating meat too."

"Now, Felicia," Luis began, rolling his eyes.

"It's just not right, Luis!" Felicia lunged to her feet. "You know somewhere in this school, someone's eating rabbit right now!"

Luis blanched and several other students at the table groaned.

Amelia wondered if that was really true or if Felicia was just being dramatic. Rabbit seemed kind of elaborate for a school lunch.

"Come on, Felicia," a boy with gray and white hair said. "Not this again."

"Why not this, Sam? We ignore it, but it's not right!"

"Wow, you're really passionate about being a vegetarian," Amelia said. Seeing Felicia get all worked up made Amelia realize she maybe wasn't as animal-friendly as she could be. After all, she didn't exactly go around trying to convince others to give up meat. She'd always just figured to each their own.

Felicia looked like she was going to say something else, but then just nodded and sat back down.

"Passionate's one word for it," Sam said.

Luis laughed. "He's right. You haven't seen anything yet."

Felicia let out a huff of exasperation, but didn't say anything.

"Don't mind them. I totally get it. I'm a vegetarian because I don't like the idea of eating animals. Still I understand why some people do. Protein's hard to find. And speaking of…" Amelia reached into her bookbag and pulled out a couple small, plastic containers. She opened the first and poured kidney beans over her salad. She then opened the second and shook out the peanut and sunflower mix she'd created that morning. Snapping the containers closed, she put them back in her bag and picked up her fork.

"What's that?" Felicia leaned over to stare at her plate.

Amelia smiled. "Kidney beans and nuts."

"Those are nuts?" Luis leaned over to stare.

"They don't look like nuts to me," Felicia said.

"Well, some are sunflowers seeds, but the rest are nuts."

"They're too small," Felicia said.

"What happened to their shells?" Sam asked.

Amelia looked at him, then back down at her salad. "They're shelled nuts. I buy them that way." Of course she'd had to request a special order at the grocery store since the only nuts they'd had in stock required a nutcracker.

"You don't eat the shells?" Luis asked.

Amelia laughed. "No way." The look on everyone's faces made her wonder though. "You don't actually eat the shells, do you?"

"Of course not!" Sam laughed. "They're just messing with you."

"Yeah." Felicia laughed. "I mean, who eats the shells?"

The redheaded kid across from them, who'd been quiet up to that point, piped up. "Well, the squirre–" He suddenly squeaked to a stop and coughed.

Amelia nodded. "Well that's true I guess. Squirrels probably would eat the shells, but I doubt any humans do." She laughed and everyone else laughed as well, but there was an air at the table she didn't quite understand. Almost as if they didn't agree with her.

Suddenly she really wanted to see the other cafeterias. This one was weird enough – so many leaves and vegetables she didn't recognize – that she was really curious to see the others. And even though Felicia seemed to think there weren't enough vegetarians at the school, there were way more here than at any school Amelia'd ever attended, though she supposed it did make a kind of weird sense, what with the entire town being an animal sanctuary. It probably wasn't too much of a jump for the residents to adopt an animal, decide not to eat that animal, then expand that thinking to include the animals adopted by all their friends. In fact, it was probably stranger to Felicia that only one of the four cafeterias was vegetarian.

"Not to completely change the subject," Felicia said, "but Paulie's really getting on Mrs. Spider's nerves in art class."

"I noticed." Amelia nodded. "She's kind of scary when she gets upset."

"That's for sure," Sam muttered.

"What'd Paulie do?" Luis asked.

"Mrs. Spider stepped out of the room last week and –" Felicia hesitated, glanced at Amelia, then continued, "for some reason, Paulie decided to climb a shelf and hang out the window and Mrs. Spider caught him."

"That was probably my fault," Amelia said. "No wonder he hates me."

"What? No way," Luis said. "Paulie gets along with everyone."

"Not with me."

"What do you mean it was your fault?" Sam asked.

"Mrs. Spider had to rescue me from Katrina," Amelia said.

Felicia gasped. "Katrina Tiger?"

Amelia nodded and then explained how Katrina had caught Amelia in the hallway on her way to art class.

The table went dead silent and Felicia looked terrified. "She had her arm around your shoulders," she whispered.

"Yeah. She wanted me to go with her, hang out I think."

Luis shook his head. "That's not good, Amelia. You should probably avoid her."

Amelia had been thinking the same thing, but hearing Luis say it kind of annoyed her. Did he think she couldn't take care of herself? "Don't be ridiculous. I mean, yeah, she was kind of intimidating, but I'm sure she's perfectly nice."

Everyone at the table was shaking their heads.

"No?"

"No," Felicia breathed. "We stay away from the ti–" She stopped abruptly.

"From the what?"

"The Tiger family. Katrina and her brother Jacob. They're scary."

"Yeah," Luis agreed. "They're – what's the word? There's a word. I know it. When someone's in high school and they're mean to all the other kids…"

"A bully?" Amelia asked.

"Yes! That's it. They're both bullies." Luis sat back, looking pleased with himself.

"I've never heard that word before," Felicia said. "It sounds almost too nice for them. Are you sure that's the right word?"

"Yes," Luis said decisively. "It's definitely the right word. Bullies."

Before Amelia could even think of a reply, the bell rang, and there was a mad rush to dump trays and get to class. It wasn't until Amelia was seated in Biology, taking notes as Mrs. Hedgehog droned on and on, that it occurred to her.

Who attended school anywhere in the United States without ever having heard the word "bully"?

six

the zombie apocalypse

AMELIA REMEMBERED LUIS' words as she entered Technology that afternoon. Her assigned spot was right between The Zone of Awkward where Paulie sat and the Zone of Scary where Katrina was.

Paulie would be much easier (and less scary) to win over than Katrina, so Amelia smiled at him as she settled into her seat.

His response was to glare at her before hunching over his keyboard and, in a repeat from art class, edging his chair away from hers.

Great.

Deciding to ignore his lack of enthusiasm, Amelia said cheerfully, "Hi, Paulie! Long time no see."

Paulie made a weird sound, something between a squeak and squawk. She couldn't really describe it. The sound reminded her of something she'd heard before, but she couldn't quite figure out what it was.

She'd heard it in the woods maybe or outside her house or ...

"Stop stare-stare-staring," Paulie snapped.

Amelia jumped. "Sorry. I didn't mean to stare. I just – never mind. So how's your day been?"

Paulie shrugged. "Work-work-work."

Well, that was a good point. Amelia sighed and turned to her computer. She pulled up the pop culture presentation she was working on and started searching the internet for zombie images.

"What the freaky furry frack is that?"

Amelia looked up.

Katrina was staring at her computer screen with a horrified look on her face.

"It's a zombie."

"What's a zombie-zombie?" Paulie asked on her other side.

What the helvetica? They didn't know what a zombie was? "You know, as in the walking dead." Hey, at least they were finally talking to her.

"That doesn't make sense. The dead can't walk." Katrina said.

"Well, technically no, but that's the whole point of zombies. If the dead could come back to life, that's what they'd look like."

"That's really disturbing," Paulie said.

Amelia shrugged. "It's the zombie apocalypse. It's supposed to be disturbing."

"What does that mean? The zombie apocalypse?" Katrina was still staring at the zombie on Amelia's screen.

She'd chosen a pretty good one. It was a man. She tilted her head. Or maybe it was a woman. Hard to tell with so many body parts destroyed. Pretty gruesome stuff. "It just means, you know, the end of the world, zombie-style."

"That's just not right." A new voice spoke from behind them. Amelia glanced over her shoulder. Oh, great. It was the freak from Calculus. The one who kept sniffing her hair.

"No one invited you to join the party, Victor." Katrina waved him away, but Victor just stood there.

"Really," he said to Amelia. "Why would anyone think the apocalypse is cool, zombie-style or not? I mean, the end of the world is kind of a downer, you know."

Amelia shrugged. "Yeah, but as long as it's just a story, no one really has to worry about it in real life. Things can always get worse. I think that's the whole point of the zombie-craze and dystopian novels and apocalyptic, end-of-the-world horror stories."

"That's a very depressing-pressing viewpoint," Paulie said.

"What's going on over here?" Mr. Fox loomed over Amelia's computer.

"Look at what the hu–mm-ummm. Hmm." Paulie cleared his throat. "Look at what Amelia-Melia's working on. She's doing a presentation on – what did you call it, call it?"

"Pop culture."

"I thought it was the zombie apocalypse," Victor said.

Amelia shook her head. "No. The zombie apocalypse is only one aspect of pop culture.There's so much more than that. Sure it's movies and music and TV, but it's also fashion and slang and belief structures."

Mr. Fox grunted. "Victor, Katrina, Paulie, get back to your seats and get to work on your own presentations. And Amelia," he glanced at her screen and blanched. "That's really disturbing."

"That's what I said!" Paulie exclaimed.

Mr. Fox shook his head. "Doesn't matter. Just keep working on your presentation. I'm sure it will be very interesting."

"Yeah," Katrina said. "I'm actually kind of looking forward to learning more about this pop culture."

Amelia rolled her eyes. It was a good thing she didn't believe in zombies because this town was absolutely dead last on the list of places to be if the zombie apocalypse ever did happen.

seven

shifter spies

"I CAN'T BELIEVE we're doing this, Paulie. This just feels weird, skulking after Amelia." Melvin worried she'd see them and want to talk. What would he do then? What if his antlers made an appearance? This was a terrible idea.

"I was right, though. She's with the bunny-bunnies!"

Amelia and Felicia walked along the sidewalk, the two of them talking animatedly, with Luis, Sam and Mason trailing behind them.

It was Paulie's idea for him and Melvin to walk on the opposite side of the street while following the four bunnies and Amelia. Paulie insisted they wouldn't be noticed from where they stood. Melvin thought it was a ridiculous plan.

"This is quill-quilled up!" Paulie said. "Look at them! I knew they were in cahoots. She probably told the bunny-bunnies all about my stash in the woods and now they're plotting to steal even more of my acorns!"

"Now, Paulie, we don't know that."

"Of course we do! What else could they possibly be talking about?"

Amelia and the bunnies turned the corner and headed toward town.

"Where are they going?" Paulie asked. "The bunny-bunnies shouldn't take her to town!"

"Why not, Paulie? This is her town too. Everyone's going to have to get used to her going pretty much wherever she wants."

"But what if she sees something she shouldn't?"

"Then she'll learn the truth, and shiftastic news – it won't be because of me and my antlers!"

"Come on, Melvin! We're losing them." Paulie darted across the street and turned the corner.

Melvin sighed and followed.

"Let's get some ice cream." Felicia turned to face Amelia and bounced backward as they walked. "Do you like ice cream, Amelia?"

"Love it."

"Awesome." Bounce-bounce. "I think it's the best thing ever." Bounce-bounce. "Well, second best thing. After carrot tops. What's your favorite flavor?"

"Oh, I don't know. It's hard to say. Pistachio maybe. Or Rocky Road."

Felicia stopped bouncing. "There's a pistachio ice cream?" she asked, wonder in her voice.

"Well, yeah."

"I don't think Shiffer Ice Cream Parlor has that flavor."

"Bummer. That's okay though. I'm sure I can find something."

"Sure. Sure." Felicia started to bounce again. "Let's hurry, okay?" She darted across the square in long bounds, Amelia racing after her.

"Where are they going now?" Paulie grumbled as he hurried across the square, trying to keep the bunnies in sight. "Hurry, Melvin-Elvin!"

They arrived at the center of the square in time to watch the bunnies disappear into the ice cream parlor.

"Well, that's just great," Melvin said.

"Oh, man. You don't think the cats are helping them, do you? Maybe they're selling my acorn-acorns to the ice cream parlor. Maybe the Siamese are working on a new flavor. Acorn ice cream! That would be so feralicious-licious!"

"I seriously doubt they're selling your acorns, Paulie."

"Well, if they are, they could have just asked. I would have given them my acorn-acorns for such a noble cause. They didn't have to steal them!"

"We still don't know if they're the ones who took your acorns, Paulie."

"Well, who else would it be? It had to be the bunny-bunnies, I'm telling you. There's no other explanation. It's the thievin', blasted bunny-bunnies!"

"Right. Well, the thievin' bunnies are inside eating ice cream while we're outside, hungry and bored. So what's the plan now, Paulie?"

"I could go get us some ice cream. Maybe I'll find out what they're up to, up to."

"Fine." Melvin stretched out on a bench and closed his eyes. "I'll be here. Waiting."

"What flavor do you want?"

Melvin cracked open one eye. "Willow."

"Always willow. You never try any of the other flavors. What if there's an amazing flavor, better even than willow? Are you sure you don't want to try –"

"Willow."

"Fine. I'll be back soon." Paulie ran across the street and peered into the ice cream parlor. The bunnies were already sitting at a table in the center of the room, eating their ice cream and talking. Not the human though. Amelia was standing at the counter, still staring into the case. Probably couldn't decide which flavor to get. Paulie totally understood that. Unlike Melvin with his obsession with Willow, Paulie had tried pretty much every flavor in the parlor, some with disastrous results. He shuddered, remembering the foul taste of spinach ice cream.

He pulled open the door and walked inside, already anticipating trying a new flavor. The parlor always had at least one new flavor he hadn't tried before and he always looked forward to discovering what it was.

Laney looked up from where she stood behind the counter and made a face at him. "Oh, it's you. What do you want?"

Paulie froze in the doorway. He hadn't even noticed that Laney was the one working the counter this afternoon. This was a totally unexpected development. No matter how much he loved ice cream, when Laney worked the counter, he chose not to indulge.

He inched backward, contemplating leaving and disappointing Melvin, when Amelia spoke up.

"Well," she said, "I suppose since it's an ice cream parlor he's probably here for some ice cream. Come on in, Paulie. Maybe you can help me choose a flavor. I've never tried any of these."

Just like that, Paulie was hooked. "Really? You've never tried any of these flavors?" He hurried to Amelia's side. "I've tried them all and I can definitely tell you which ones are the best-best-best and which ones you might want to avoid."

Laney gasped. "As if we would have any flavors that aren't absolutely delicious, Paulie Porcupine. Just because your taste buds aren't fully developed doesn't mean–"

"So you've tried the spinach ice cream then?" Paulie asked. He didn't know where he'd suddenly found the courage to speak like that to Laney. Maybe it was Amelia. She'd stood up to Laney and suddenly he wasn't so afraid of her anymore. If a human had the courage to speak out, so should he. "You liked it then?"

Laney made a face.

"I've tried them all," Paulie repeated. "Have you?" He knew the answer of course. She'd never risk trying anything but her favorites.

Laney huffed. "Just choose your flavors already."

"I'm not sure there's anything here I'm ready to try," Amelia said.

"Oh, come on," Paulie said. "Be brave. The worst thing that can happen is you'll hate-hate it. And then you'll just throw it away. But at least you'll know not to choose that flavor next time."

Amelia laughed. "Okay, I guess I'll try a multi-flavored scoop."

Paulie blanched. Should he warn her? He was pretty sure human taste buds wouldn't be the same as his. Maybe she'd like the combination of flavors.

"And I'll take a scoop of willow-willow and a scoop of…" Paulie scanned the cases. "Forest Trail-Trails." That sounded interesting. He could ask Laney what was in the ice cream, but she probably wouldn't tell him. The parlor was like that, keeping their ingredients secret, so no one could steal their recipes. So he'd just make it a game, taste and guess, taste and guess, like always.

"I suppose the willow's for that idiot moo-Melvin," Laney said.

Paulie didn't answer, just handed her some money and took his scoops. He headed for the door.

"Hey, Paulie, you can join us," Amelia said.

"Nah, gotta get back to Melvin-Elvin."

Amelia's eyes lit up. "Oh. Well, tell him I said hi, and you know, you're both welcome to join us. If you want."

"Thanks. I'll let him know that." It wasn't until Paulie had reached the square that he realized he'd forgotten entirely his whole mission in going into the ice cream parlor in the first place. He was supposed to find out what they were up to, figure out where'd they'd taken his acorns, if they were selling them at the parlor. He sighed. Oh, well. He'd figure it out later. After he'd eaten his Forest Trails ice cream.

eight

multi flavors

AMELIA SAT BETWEEN Felicia and Mason, the red-headed kid from lunch earlier that day. She'd finally figured out his name.

"So Paulie was pretty friendly just now," Felicia said.

"Yeah, didn't seem like he really hated you at all," Luis said.

Amelia nodded. "I know. It's weird. He blows hot and cold, all friendly one minute, then glaring and ignoring me the next. I don't know what his deal is. I'm also not sure about this ice cream." It was a weird color. Light brown and it looked like it had thin strands of something in it. She remembered Paulie's advice and smiled.

One tiny taste wouldn't hurt, right?

She lifted the spoon and already had a bite in her mouth before the smell hit her. Was that –

She inadvertently swallowed and gagged.

No way.

She lifted the cup and sniffed. Yes. It was definitely fishy.

"Hey, Laney," she called over her shoulder.

"What do you want?"

"What's in the multi-flavored scoop anyway?"

"None of your business. It's our bestselling flavor and we're not giving away our trade secrets, just so you can go make your own and never have to come here again. You can just forget it."

Amelia raised an eyebrow. "Well, there's no risk of me ever wanting to make this on my own." She shoved the cup away.

"Paulie's tried all the flavors in here," Sam told her.

"Yeah, he mentioned that."

"He's made it a kind of game to identify what's in each flavor. I'm pretty sure he said that one was a mix of tuna, salmon and catfish."

Amelia gagged. "That is so gross."

"It's really popular with the cat–" Felicia stopped, a guilty look on her face.

Amelia laughed. "Yeah, my dad gets mad at me when I let the cats eat my ice cream too. But come on. They're cats. It's dairy. They can hardly resist, right? And I imagine if I brought this home they'd be all over it. I have no idea how any human could find it edible though, even if they love fish." She looked around suspiciously. "Are you guys sure this is a people ice cream parlor? I mean, it kind of reminds of those really fancy dog bakeries."

Luis laughed. "Nah. It's for people. I guess we just have some really interesting flavors. It takes some getting used to, but eventually you'll find the flavors you love and they won't be like anything else you've ever tried."

"If you say so." Amelia kind of doubted they'd ever have a flavor she considered palatable. The options had all been truly weird. Bamboo

Goodness, Rocky Shrubs, Salty Bark. She eyed everyone else at the table.

Felicia had chosen Veggie Delight while Luis had chosen Pine Cone Crunch. She hadn't caught the flavors Sam and Mason chose, but she was pretty certain they were just as weird.

Oh, well. She hadn't really wanted ice cream anyway. She'd just been glad to be included in this after-school outing.

"So what do you want to do now?" Felicia asked, bouncing in her chair.

"What do you guys usually do after school?"

"Homework," they all chorused.

"We don't usually do much on school nights," Luis explained. "We mostly go to the library to study."

"Because it's too loud in our homes," Sam said.

"Loud?" Amelia asked.

Mason rolled his eyes. "We all have little brothers and sisters."

"Oh." Amelia was an only child, so she couldn't even imagine what it must be like to have younger siblings running around. Before she could ask any questions, Felicia suddenly bounded out of her chair.

"I know, I know, I know!" she squealed. "Let's go bowling!"

Everyone's eyes swung to Amelia. "Um. Okay." She was kind of surprised they wanted to bowl. "Every time I stop by, though, no one's there."

"That makes it all the better!" Luis said. "We can bowl and study and no one will bother us."

"Okay." Amelia stood. "I'm game if you guys are."

nine

the bowling alley

"MELVIN-MELVIN, THEY'RE coming out of the ice cream parlor."

"Great. Let me know when they do something suspicious." Melvin wasn't really interested in following Amelia or the bunnies anymore. After his scoop of willow ice cream, he'd done some homework, then stretched back out on the bench. He was ready for another nap.

"No, really, Melvin, we gotta follow them."

"Are they leaving the square?"

"Um. I don't know yet."

"Well, until they leave the square, we really don't have to move. We can see if they go into any building on the square from here. So I'm not moving until I have to."

"Fine-fine-fine. You stay there. I'll be back."

Melvin didn't know how much time had passed, but it seemed only a few minutes before Paulie was back.

"You're not going to believe where they went, Melvin!"

"Where?"

"The bowling alley!"

At that, Melvin opened his eyes. Everyone was pretty curious about the bowling alley, but so far, every time the human had visited it, she'd left again, almost immediately.

The Town Council was starting to think they'd wasted their money putting in a bowling alley when neither human seemed interested in spending time inside it. It was a pretty big building to waste on something that wasn't being used.

"Did they come right back out like usual?"

"No, they stayed inside!"

"Really?" Melvin sat up. "What are they doing in there?"

Paulie shrugged."I don't know. We need to find out, Melvin. This is huge!"

It really kind of was. Melvin was as curious as everyone else in town. "Okay. Let's go. It's a big enough building, if we go up the outside stairs and go in that way, we can watch from the balcony above, and they'll never even know we were there."

"Are you guys sure it's okay for us to be in here?" Amelia asked. "I mean the lights are all off."

"Yeah, just give me a minute." Sam disappeared around the corner and a couple minutes later, the lights started coming on all over the building.

"Come on!" Felicia grabbed Amelia's arm and dragged her down a couple steps toward the lanes. "How does it work? Do we all get our own alley?"

"What?"

"You know. This is alley 1 and that's alley 2. Do we each get our own?"

"Oh, um, actually they're called lanes. The whole place is the alley, but each of these are lanes. And no, we don't all get our own. There are five of us, so we can all play on one lane if we want. Or we can split and have two on one lane and three on another. Or we can have two lanes and all five of us play on both, so we get to bowl more often." Amelia looked around. "No one's here though. I mean to take our money."

"What do you mean, take our money? There's no charge to use the bowling alley." Luis sat at one of the stations and started pushing buttons. "What does this do?"

"That's where you keep score. You guys have never bowled before?"

"Nope." Sam plopped down on a chair. "So you get to teach us all."

"Okay. Well first we need shoes."

"We have shoes," Mason said.

"Yeah, but not these shoes. We need special shoes so we don't slide on the lanes. Come on." Amelia led them up to the front counter, where sure enough there were a ton of shoes in cubbies behind the counter. "Are you sure we can just help ourselves?"

"Oh, yeah, definitely," Luis said, heading behind the counter. "So let's see, what sizes?"

A few minutes later, everyone had shoes they were changing into.

"Now what?" Felicia popped up and bounced in her shoes. "They're kind of cute. In a weird, not-cute way."

Amelia laughed. "I know, right? Now, we need to get a bowling ball. Come on." She led the way and after much hefting and practicing, they had each chosen a ball.

"Me first, me first," Felicia bounced up and down. "I can't wait."

"Um, maybe you should let Amelia go first," Luis said.

"No, that's okay," Amelia assured him.

"Yeah, but she's never done this before. None of us have," Sam said.

"I'm not even sure we know what we're supposed to do," Mason said.

"Good point. Okay, Amelia, you go first. I'll go after you!" Felicia grinned.

"Well, I'm not a very good bowler, just so you know. I'll probably teach you guys all wrong, but basically your job is to roll the ball down the lane and knock down as many pins as you can." She quickly stepped up to the line and demonstrated, sending her ball rolling down the lane where it knocked over two pins.

"Yay! You won, Amelia!" Felicia jumped up and down.

"Not really. The goal is to knock down all ten. I only got two. But the good news is I get a second try. Everyone gets two tries to knock down the ten pins." She tossed a second ball and watched it gutter pretty quickly. "See what I mean? Not the best bowler. Your turn, Felicia."

Felicia's first try involved the bowling ball skipping two lanes to crash into the barrier three lanes over. "Oh, my gosh! I didn't mean to do that!"

And things progressed downward from there.

Sam and Mason had a tendency to launch the balls so they flew through the air before crashing to the ground with a massive thud and then barreling over a couple pins on their way down the lane. They did a pretty good job of keeping their throws to the center of the lane. Unfortunately, they launched the balls with such force they rarely knocked over more than four pins at a time and inevitably ended up causing a split that resulted in no pins down on their second throws.

Luis was determined to match Amelia's style by ensuring the ball ran the course of the lane from start to finish, rather than going airborne. The result was he guttered about seventeen times before finally managing to knock down one pin.

Felicia's enthusiasm only grew as the night wore on and she tended to bounce at the exact moment she tossed her ball, which meant it never landed in their lane. Instead, it landed and barreled toward pins that were one, two and even three lanes over from where they were bowling. Amelia ended up activating all the lanes so that Felicia's balls had a chance to knock down pins wherever they landed.

Paulie snickered as Felicia's ball guttered three lanes over from where she was standing. "I don't think she's supposed to be doing it that way, do you?"

Melvin laughed. "Doubtful. Actually I'm not sure any of them know what they're doing. But it looks fun."

"It does, doesn't it? We should go-go-go and join them, Melvin."

"Do you seriously think my moose can handle being in the same room with Amelia and Felicia? I'll be all antlered out for sure."

"True. You could try shifting up here. You know, like you did last week."

"No way. I felt so sick afterward and then I couldn't call my moose when I needed him. No, I'll just keep avoiding her."

"She likes you, though. She likes both of us. She wanted us to join them in the ice cream parlor. I told her no, of course, but she really wanted to see you. Maybe you should try–"

"No, okay? No."

"Okay, I get it, but what if we could figure out the timing?"

"What do you mean?"

"I mean we practice on the weekends to figure out how long you lose your moose for and then we time it so you don't get all antler-antlered out in the mornings, but by afternoon, your moose is back in time for P.E."

Melvin stared at Paulie. "That's actually not a bad plan. Still, I hate crippling my moose like that. I felt horrible afterward."

"I know. It's up to you. I guess it just depends on how much you want to know Amelia-Melia."

Quite a lot was the answer to that. "I'll think about it. So can we go now, Paulie? Our homework's completely finished and all we're doing is standing around watching other people have fun." They'd been hanging out on the second floor of the building for a couple hours now. It wasn't a bad spot. Quiet, with tables and comfortable couches and chairs for lounging. And a perfect view from the balcony of the bowling alley below. Still, Melvin was ready for dinner.

"I haven't found my acorns yet, though."

"Maybe you should just ask them."

"Ask them? I couldn't possibly. Besides they'd probably just lie-lie-lie."

Melvin sighed. "Or maybe they didn't take them."

"They did, they did! I know they did. No one else knew where my stash was. Just Amelia-Melia."

"Okay. So what's the plan?"

Paulie scowled.

"You don't have a plan, do you?"

"Not really. Fine. Let's just go."

"Finally." Melvin led the way out of the building. He was halfway down the stairs when the doors opened below them and the bunnies and Amelia spilled out on the sidewalk laughing. Melvin froze. *Don't look up. Don't look up.*

As if she'd heard his thoughts, Amelia looked up, her bright blue eyes causing his heart to stutter.

A delighted smile crossed her face. "Melvin! Paulie!"

Melvin clapped both hands to his head, swung around and raced back up the stairs, pushing past Paulie and barreling back into the bowling alley.

One antler sprang free and the combined force of his lurching run and its weight pulled him to the left. He tripped over his own feet, crashed into a couch and the second antler broke free.

The added weight pulled him over the back of the couch and he landed half on the couch, half on the floor, ears ringing, head pounding.

Groaning, he reached up and grabbed his antlers, holding them still, desperate to make the ringing and pounding stop.

"Where'd Melvin go?"

Holy scat! That was Amelia and she sounded really close. They weren't coming up here, were they? Melvin lurched to his feet, holding his head tilted back a bit so he wouldn't overbalance. He looked around the room frantically.

"What's your problem, Paulie?" That sounded like Felicia and she was right outside the back door! She'd keep Amelia out, wouldn't she? Melvin caught sight of the bar on the other side of the room. He raced toward it, flung up the counter and slid behind the bar. The counter slapped closed and the back door began to open.

Melvin flung himself down, landing hard on his knees. He scooted as close to the bar as he could get, braced his back against it and crouched as low as possible. One roll of his eyes upward told him him it wasn't low enough. His antlers were just too tall for the bar and there wasn't enough room for him to stretch out on the floor.

Maybe she wouldn't notice them. Or maybe she'd think they were shed antlers. Or maybe he was dewlapped.

ten

the enemy

"WHERE'D MELVIN GO?" Amelia asked, climbing the stairs toward Paulie. She was so tired of Melvin running away every time she saw him.

Paulie didn't answer. He was busy glaring over Amelia's shoulder.

Amelia looked behind her, but it was just Felicia and the guys.

Felicia must have noticed him glaring. "What's your problem, Paulie?"

"You know what my problem is and I don't appreciate you using the huuu-help of Amelia for your own nefarious-farious purposes."

Felicia looked shocked. "I don't know what you're talking about. What nefarious purposes?"

"Don't pretend like you don't know what you did!"

Felicia shook her head in confusion.

"And you!" Paulie turned on Amelia. "Acting all friendly-friendly, like we're the best of friends, then plotting away with the bunny-bunnies." He sneered at them.

"Hey," Luis straightened up from where he was leaning against the rail. He caught in one hand the acorns he'd been juggling and glared at Paulie. "Don't be a jerk."

"Oh, like you're so innocent. You're one of them! You're the enemy, you're all the enemy-enemy!" Waving his arms in the air, Paulie pushed his way through them and stormed down the stairs, muttering as he went. "Thievin' blasted bunny-bunnies, can't be trus-trusted…"

A beat of silence followed Paulie's exit. Amelia had no idea what had just happened. It seemed that was the story of her life lately. Every conversation she had anymore felt like she was missing vital pieces of information. "What was that all about? He was fine in the ice cream parlor!"

Felicia shrugged. "Who knows? Paulie's always been a little odd. Let's go, okay?"

Amelia shook her head. "No, I want to see where Melvin went. Come on." She climbed the last of the stairs and opened the door.

"Maybe we should go after Paulie. You know, he seemed pretty angry." Sam sounded worried.

"Yeah, just like a chittering–" Mason stopped.

"Chittering!" Amelia stopped two steps inside the room and swung back around. "That's what it sounded like earlier."

"What?" Felicia stepped inside and looked around the room.

"Paulie made a sound in tech class. It was just like the chittering of a squirrel that I hear every morning outside my window. The squirrel's always yelling at the birds for something. It's really funny and Paulie sounded just like one."

"Oh, I'm sure you're just imagining it," Luis said. "Hey, this room is pretty cool."

"Yeah," Sam said. "We could totally come here and study. Better even than the library."

"Who cares about the room? I'm telling you he sounded just like a squirrel. If I didn't know his last name was Porcupine, I'd think Paulie's family had adopted the squirrel instead."

Felicia looked at Luis, who shrugged. "Well actually," she said, "some of his family did adopt the squirrel."

"They did?"

"Yep." Mason popped up from behind a couch. Amelia wondered what he'd been doing back there. "A lot of the families in town adopt more than one animal. Just depends on the family."

"Paulie's family adopted the porcupine and the squirrel," Sam said.

"So is that what the families do then? Study their adopted animals and practice sounding like them, acting like them?"

"Um, sure," Felicia said brightly. "It's fun, you know."

Amelia wasn't so sure about that, but to each their own. "So that's why you're always hopping?"

Felicia froze, her heels slightly off the ground, her upward motion arrested by the question.

"Yep," Luis said, slinging his arm around his sister's shoulders. "That and she's got lots of energy."

"You do it too," Amelia said. "So do Sam and Mason."

"Sure. It's great exercise. Plus I figure our families adopted the rabbit, we should represent you know."

"Represent?"

"Oh, yeah," Felicia said. "Because everyone's always complaining about the little animals, especially the bunnies. Just because they like to eat people's gardens, they're called pests. Well, bunnies have to eat too!" Felicia huffed and crossed her arms.

"It's true," Luis agreed, nodding. "No one likes the bunnies."

"Except other bunnies," Sam said.

"Well I like bunnies," Amelia declared.

"And that's why we like you, Amelia!" Felicia and Luis chorused.

Everyone laughed.

eleven

in plain sight

FOR THE LOVE of dewlaps. Were they never going to leave? What was wrong with these shifter bunnies? They needed to be convincing Amelia to leave the bowling alley, not hanging around, chatting all afternoon.

Movement in Melvin's peripheral vision made him freeze. He couldn't tell who it was. *Please don't let it be Amelia. Please don't let it be Amelia.*

Sam's grinning face popped over the top of the bar and Melvin relaxed.

Sam winked and disappeared again.

Melvin hoped that meant he was going to encourage Amelia to leave, but instead Melvin heard him say, "Hey, Amelia, come look at this."

For hooves' sake, he wasn't bringing her over here, was he?

"What is it?" Amelia's voice got further away.

"Not sure. Looks like some kind of game." At least Sam was taking her further away, but why wasn't he getting her out of the bowling alley?

"Oh, that's a pinball machine! Gosh, I haven't played one of these in forever. Is it plugged in?"

Silence, then, "Now it is!"

A series of chimes and dings sounded and Felicia squealed.

Melvin winced.

"Show us how to play, Amelia, please!"

Amelia laughed. "Okay."

After that, all Melvin heard was a series of dings and exclamations from the others.

Suddenly Sam was there, lifting the countertop away. "Come on, quick, while they're busy with the pinball thing," he whispered.

Melvin carefully stood and sent a wary glance over to the corner where all the noise was coming from. He couldn't even see Amelia. Luis, Mason and Felicia were crowded around her, blocking his view.

Melvin quickly exited the bar area. "Thanks, Sam," he muttered as he passed him by.

Sam grinned. "You bet."

Melvin raced to the door and had just opened it when he heard Felicia squeal again. He glanced over his shoulder.

Felicia was jumping up and down and clapping her hands. Amelia was laughing and Mason and Luis were arguing over whose turn it was next. Sam was headed back toward them, looking like he'd probably join the argument any minute.

Melvin sighed, stepped outside and let the door close behind him. He loped down the stairs and hurried around to the back of the building. He had three choices.

One, walk home with his antlers out and proud.

Not even an option.

Two, shift completely into his moose form.

Or three, try and force his antlers back into submission.

After multiple attempts proved his antlers were going nowhere, Melvin stripped and shifted. He then clumped along the edges of the town square, keeping to the shadows of the buildings as much as possible, hoping no one noticed the big-rumped moose wandering down Main Street.

When he finally reached his house, he found a porcupine waiting on the porch. Melvin shifted in the yard, pulled out his clothes and dressed quickly, all the while glaring at Paulie. "I can't believe you abandoned me."

Paulie just sat there staring at him.

"I mean, seriously, Paulie. You knew my antlers were out. You knew she was going to try and catch me. And you knew there was only one way out of that room. Yet you left me behind. Just abandoned your post. What if she'd seen my antlers?"

Paulie just stared.

Melvin huffed and stormed inside the house.

Paulie didn't follow.

Melvin held open the door. "Well, come on already."

Paulie stood, but instead of going inside, he walked down the front steps and waddled across the yard toward the woods.

"Fine! Be that way!" Melvin slammed the door.

"Who are you yelling at, sweetheart?"

"Oh, sorry, Mom. It was just Paulie. Making me crazy as usual."

"That's weird. I thought Paulie was upstairs in your room." She shrugged. "Oh well."

Melvin stood there a moment, then ran up to his room. He flung open the door and sure enough, there was Paulie sprawled across his giant moose-sized bed. Melvin slammed the door. "Have you been here all along?"

Paulie sat up. "Yeah. Sorry-sorry-sorry. Their innocent act makes me crazy. Can you believe Felicia and Amelia pretended they didn't even know why I was so upset, when all the while Luis was standing there juggling my acorn-acorns right in front of me? I was so crazy-mad, I completely forgot you were inside, all antler-antlered up. I didn't mean to leave you. I was halfway home before I remembered. Then I came here, but you weren't here yet. I was a little worried, but I figured the bunny-bunnies, for all their faults, would keep Amelia-Melia away."

"Ha!" Melvin collapsed in his armchair. "That's what you think."

"The bunny-bunnies let her see your antlers?"

"Well, no, but only because I managed to hide before she walked in!" And Melvin proceeded to tell him everything that had happened since Paulie left him at the bowling alley, from being forced to hide with his antlers in plain sight to Sam helping him escape. He even shared about having to walk home as a moose.

He didn't tell Paulie about mistaking him for a full-blooded porcupine though.

He was pretty certain Paulie wouldn't take that well.

"We need a new plan," Paulie said unexpectedly.

"What are you talking about?"

"Weren't you listening? They obviously have my acorn-acorns and are just tormenting me! We need a plan for figuring out where they hid-

hid-hid them!"

"Oh, Paulie."

"Tomorrow, we're going on an acorn hunt, Melvin. If it's the last thing I do, I'm finding my acorns and I'm taking them back from those blasted, thievin' bunny-bunnies!"

twelve

the tiger plan

MELVIN OPENED HIS door the next morning and almost ran over Paulie who was poised to ring the doorbell. "Paulie! What's up?"

"I've figured out how we're going to make this happen, Melvin. Come on!" Paulie turned and darted down the stairs.

"What do you mean?" Melvin closed the door behind him and raced after him. "Paulie, hold up. What are you talking about?"

"My acorns, of course!"

"What about them?"

"I've figured out how we're going to find them."

"Okay, tell me how."

"The tigers!"

"You mean Jake and Katrina?"

"Do you know any other tigers? Of course, Jake and Katrina! They're tigers. That means they're masters of stealth. They can follow the bunny-bunnies and no one will see them. I'm going to bury some more acorns while the tigers follow the bunny-bunnies. I'll hide by my stash, the tigers will follow the bunnies, and when they try to steal my stash, we'll pounce."

"Uh, what does that mean? Pounce?" Melvin had a sudden vision of Jake in tiger form mauling Felicia's fragile bunny. It wasn't a pretty sight.

"On the acorns, to keep them from stealing more of them! And on the bunnies, to force them to tell me where my other acorns are and get them back for me!"

"So your plan is to use the tigers to torture the bunnies?"

"Well…"

"You do know that Jake and Katrina have a hard enough time suppressing their animal instincts without you riling them up and sending them out to hunt bunnies."

"But–"

"No, Paulie. This is not a good idea. Not at all!"

"I don't want them to hurt them. Just maybe scare them a little. So they'll tell us where my acorns are. I'll make sure the tiger-tigers understand the plan."

"And when the bunnies have heart attacks because the tigers scare them to death? Or when one of the tigers loses control and ends up committing murder? Is that all going to be according to the plan, Paulie?"

"Why do you always have to assume the water trough is half-empty, Melvin? Maybe it's half-full!"

"Or maybe there's no water at all, Paulie! Maybe it's a drought and we're all going to die of thirst!"

Paulie huffed. "Whatever."

"Listen, we'll figure things out. Without involving the tigers. Okay?"

"I thought you liked Jake and Katrina."

"Sure I like them just fine. I also understand they're massive predators that I'd rather not tangle with. And Paulie, if my big-rumped moose doesn't want to tangle with the tigers, you shouldn't even consider throwing the bunnies at them."

"Fine. What are we going to do then?"

"Just what you said earlier. You'll bury some more acorns, we'll hide and watch the spot and when the bunnies arrive to steal them, we'll catch them in the act. There will be no pouncing though. Understood?"

Paulie sighed. "Fine. That doesn't sound half as fun though. When are we going to do this?"

"Might as well get it over with. Tonight after school?"

"Awesome!"

thirteen

the squirrel

WHEN AMELIA WALKED into history the next morning, the first person she saw was Katrina Tiger.

Slouched in a chair at the back of the room, Katrina looked as out of place in the classroom as any student Amelia had ever seen. How had she missed the fact that Katrina was in history with her all this time?

"Hi, Katrina," she said brightly, walking toward her.

Katrina looked up, her orange eyes reflecting eerily under the fluorescent lights. "Amelia." Her voice was a quiet rumble that sent a shiver down Amelia's spine.

"How's it going?" Amelia plopped into the seat beside Katrina, ignoring the visceral need to put several rows of desks between them.

Katrina grunted.

An awkward pause followed.

Amelia busied herself pulling out her pen and history notebook.

She opened it to a new page and carefully printed the date. Then without really thinking about it, she began doodling in the margins of the page, drawing first a backpack, then an antler, then a squirrel standing on its hind legs, chittering at a bird. She added a bubble next to the squirrel and inside the bubble, she wrote, "Leave my acorns alone, you thief!"

"Hey, Amelia!" Luis settled beside her and stared, eyebrows raised, as if demanding to know why she was seated back here, next to Katrina. Like she hadn't seen him hanging by the classroom door, popping his head in to stare at the two of them, then withdrawing to pace the hallway, only to repeat the same actions a few moments later.

"Hi, Luis. Glad you finally decided to join us."

Luis blushed.

Amelia grinned.

"Luis."

Amelia was looking right at Luis when Katrina said his name.

His eyes widened and a panicked look crossed his face before disappearing. He swallowed, leaned forward to look around Amelia and said quietly, "Hey, Katrina."

Katrina bared her teeth at him in the semblance of a smile, but even Amelia could tell, it wasn't a very nice one.

Luis sat back, an unsettled look on his face.

"Cut it out, Katrina." Luis would never believe she wasn't dangerous at this rate.

Katrina straightened from her slouch. "What?"

"You know what. Stop intimidating him."

Katrina rolled her eyes. "Whatever."

Amelia turned to Luis, who was staring at her, mouth agape.

"What?"

He shook his head. "Nothing. I just – um. Thanks, I guess."

Amelia shrugged. "Katrina's all right. You just have to get past her prickly exterior. Right, Katrina?" Amelia didn't even know what she was saying. She actually found Katrina terrifying, but everyone's attitudes at lunch the day before had made her determined to get to know her. She couldn't be that bad, right?

"Whatever you say, hum–oring you now."

"Hey, cute squirrel." Luis leaned over to stare at her picture. "Kind of reminds me of–" He stopped, a weird look on his face.

Amelia was getting tired of that – of people never finishing their sentences. "Reminds you of what?"

"A squirrel I know – I mean, not know because who can know the squirrels?" He laughed, a little nervously Amelia thought. "Just a squirrel that likes to hang out in my backyard."

"Yeah, I have one too. He's always yelling at the birds for some reason, probably because they keep stealing his acorns."

fourteen

avoiding amelia

MELVIN PEEKED AROUND the corner. The bell had rung five minutes before and Mr. Sloth still hadn't released his first class.

The rest of Melvin's class was waiting in the hallway, talking quietly.

Melvin, however, was waiting clear down the hall and around the corner, in a desperate bid to avoid Amelia.

The last time he'd run into her outside history had been a disaster. Not wanting to repeat those events for anything, Melvin waited in the opposite direction from where he knew Amelia needed to go.

If only Mr. Sloth would release class already.

Finally! The history door opened and students started pouring out. As soon as each student reached the hallway, they bolted, tearing down the halls and around corners, in a dead run for their next class.

Melvin shook his head. They were already late. Why run?

Finally, Amelia emerged, Luis one one side, Katrina on the other.

For hooves' sake, what was Katrina doing with Amelia?

A desperate urge to race over and pull Amelia away from the tiger filled Melvin, but he forced it back.

Katrina wasn't bad. Sure, she was a predator and acted all tough, but that didn't mean she'd really hurt Amelia. Katrina had spent her entire life battling her feral urges. She wouldn't give into them over a human.

What were they doing? Why weren't they moving on? "Get to class already," he hissed.

Instead, the three of them stood there, talking. What on earth could a human and two shifters, one a bunny and the other a tiger, have to talk about?

"You should totally join us for bowling after school tonight, Katrina."

Luis frantically shook his head at Amelia behind Katrina's back, but Amelia ignored him.

"Bowling?"

"Yeah, it was so much fun, we made plans to go bowling again tonight. You should absolutely come along. I promise it'll be a ton of fun." Amelia wasn't really sure that was true, especially with the look on Luis' face. He actually looked like he might faint, but Amelia was determined to prove to Luis that Katrina was just another teen like them.

"You went to the bowling alley last night." Katrina turned and stared at Luis.

He blushed. "We did."

"You bowled?"

"Yeah. Amelia taught us how. It was pretty fun." Luis glanced at

Amelia.

She widened her eyes at him and made a keep it up gesture with her hand.

"You really should join us. We're not very good at it yet, but we had a lot of fun."

"Please, Katrina?"

Katrina sighed. "Fine. When?"

"Right after school. Meet us in the courtyard. We'll walk to town, maybe get a snack, then go to the alley, okay?"

"Yeah. Gotta go." Katrina turned and loped away.

"Mrs. Spider's going to kill me," Amelia said.

Luis blanched. "Yeah, you'd better hurry. See you at lunch." He hurried after Katrina. "Hey, wait up! I need you to protect me from Mr. Grizzly!"

Finally!

Katrina left, then Luis and Amelia split apart, Luis chasing after Katrina, which was kind of weird, now that Melvin thought about it. Weren't all the bunnies afraid of Jake and Katrina? Not important though. The hallway was finally clear.

Melvin waited another minute, just to be certain Amelia wouldn't be coming back and then he bolted to Mr. Sloth's door. He jerked it open, stepped inside and closed it behind him.

Mr. Sloth paused mid-sentence and slowly turned to face Melvin. "Mr. Moose," he said slowly. "You are late."

"Sorry, Mr. Sloth. I had to avoid Amelia."

"Avoid Amelia? Why would you want to avoid a pretty girl? In my day, pretty girls were for chasing, not avoiding."

The class laughed.

Melvin could feel his face heating up.

"Unless you prefer to chase pretty boys. Which is just fine, if you do."

More snickers from the class.

Melvin felt as if his face was on fire."No, sir. I just had to avoid Amelia, you know, because she's human."

"Human? A human girl? Here? At Shifter High? You must be mistaken. Why there's never been a human in a shifter town in the history of the world, Mr. Moose."

Melvin glanced at the class and saw a lot of surprised faces looking back at him. "Well, I think we're making history then, Mr. Sloth. Amelia is a human. Remember? Her dad is our new town vet?"

"Oh, that's right. I forgot. That's actually pretty exciting. I bet we could learn a lot about humans and human history from this girl. Amelia, you said?"

'Yes, but Mr. Sloth, she doesn't know about shifters. We have to keep it a secret. That's why I was avoiding her."

"Oh, right. Yes, yes. The secret of shifters. Yes. We'll keep that secret. Like we always do. Very well, Mr. Moose. Have a seat, why don't you?"

"Thank you, sir." Melvin settled at a desk and Mr. Sloth got back to his lecture, a long and drawn-out, very detailed explanation of the role shifters played in World War II. Which didn't make sense, now that Melvin thought about it.

If Mr. Sloth truly didn't know Amelia was a human, she would already know the truth because he would have already let the truth slip about a thousand times in his endless lectures. Melvin stared at Mr.

Sloth, who glanced up from his history book, sent Melvin a quick smirk, then ducked his head and continued his lecture.

Holy scat.

Mr. Sloth had just scammed them all.

fifteen

tiger by the tail

AMELIA OPENED THE door and stepped inside the art classroom. It was quiet with everyone working on their art.

Mrs. Spider stood beside a student toward the back of the room, giving him advice on his painting.

Amelia collected her drawing from the day before, some carving tools and a wooden block. She then headed for a table at the back of the room. She settled the block of wood in front of her, picked a tool and began to carve away pieces of the wood. She was so engrossed in her work, it took her a couple minutes to realize someone stood beside her.

She glanced up.

It was Mrs. Spider.

"Oh, hello, Mrs. Spider. I'm so sorry I was late. I had to ask Katrina something after class and lost track of time. I promise it won't happen again. Well, it probably will because of Mr. Sloth, but I'll save my questions for later."

Mrs. Spider had a surprised look on her face. "Katrina Tiger?"

Amelia nodded. "I wanted to invite her to go bowling with us."

A couple gasps sounded, but when Amelia looked around, no one was paying them any attention.

"Well. That was certainly very nice of you. You like to bowl then?"

Amelia nodded. Why was everyone so surprised when she mentioned bowling? Maybe they weren't supposed to use the bowling alley after all.

But Mrs. Spider just said, "It's good that someone's finally using that building. Now talk to me about your carving."

So Amelia explained her vision. She'd never really attempted to work with wood before, but every time she thought of what medium she wanted to create her moose in, wood seemed the right choice.

Mrs. Spider appeared to agree. "I'm looking forward to seeing the final result."

Amelia was about to respond when movement caught her eye outside the window.

Was that –

Amelia stood, but suddenly, there were a bunch of kids between her and the window, the blinds had snapped closed and it was too late to figure out exactly what she was seeing.

It seemed as if every student suddenly needed Mrs. Spider's attention all at once, each of them clamoring for help with this painting or that piece of jewelry.

It was total chaos for a few minutes until Mrs. Spider clapped her hands and said, "All right, everyone. Back to your seats, right now!"

As the class settled down and got back to normal, Amelia sat frozen in her chair.

Either she was going crazy, or she'd seriously just seen a tiger racing across the school lawn with a bunny on its back and another hanging tight to its tail.

sixteen

conspiracy

AMELIA SPENT THE rest of the day thinking about that tiger. She brought it up at lunch, asking Felicia if she'd seen the tiger too, but after a beat of silence, Felicia had just laughed and asked what she'd eaten for breakfast that day.

It wasn't a hallucination!

Since Felicia had been in art class with her, she was pretty sure Felicia knew exactly what she was talking about. Why wouldn't she just admit it?

Amelia started to push the subject, but the looks on her friends' faces – like they were worried she'd lost touch with reality – made her stop.

She wasn't crazy!

She couldn't have been the only one who'd seen that tiger.

She'd desperately wanted to storm across the room and open those blinds, just to see, to get a second look, but the expression on Mrs.

Spider's face had been nothing short of terrifying.

Amelia wasn't certain why Mrs. Spider had been so angry. Maybe because all the students were out of their seats. Or maybe she was worried about the tiger racing around on school grounds. Or maybe she was still mad that Amelia had been late to class. Whatever the reason, the look on her teacher's face had kept Amelia frozen in her seat until the end of class, when she'd scurried out of the room and practically ran down the hall to English.

Halfway through her flight, she'd stopped and bolted into a classroom that wasn't even her own . She'd ignored all the kids staring at her in her mad rush to the window to stare outside. Of course, there were no tigers on the lawn by then.

She'd left and continued her journey to English class, where everyone had whispered and stared at her, like they thought she was crazy.

After English she'd come to lunch where even her friends had acted the same way.

Were they all lying to her? Conspiring to keep her from learning the truth about this school and this town? It seemed completely paranoid, but what other explanation could there possibly be? She refused to believe that she was going crazy! And if she wasn't going crazy, then there really had been a tiger and there really had been two bunnies clinging to its back and tail. But what exactly did that even mean? What was the truth the students were hiding from her? She already knew the town was an animal sanctuary. If a tiger got loose somehow, why wouldn't they just admit it?

In tech, she mentioned it to Katrina. She figured if anyone would know about a tiger on the loose, it'd be the one with the tiger-striped hair. But Katrina just stared at her before returning her eyes to her own computer screen. That was just like her. In some ways, Amelia respected Katrina's response more than anyone else's. At least, she didn't lie to Amelia or pretend she was crazy. She just refused to talk about it.

By the end of the day, Amelia was exhausted. She just wanted to go home and hide under her covers for the entire weekend, pretend she hadn't moved to this crazy town with all its weirdness.

When Amelia got to her locker, though, she found Katrina waiting for her.

"Bowling, right?" Katrina said.

Awesome. Amelia had completely forgotten she'd invited Katrina to join her and the gang for bowling. In fact, she'd forgotten about bowling entirely.

Before she could try to beg off, Felicia, Luis, Mason and Sam all arrived in a bouncing rush.

"Hi, Amelia!" Felicia bounced. "Ready for some bowling fun?"

Amelia grabbed her backpack, shoved a couple books into her locker and closed it. "I'm ready." She turned so she could see Felicia's reaction. "Katrina's going to join us."

It wasn't very nice, but Amelia took fierce satisfaction in the way the blood drained from Felicia's face and the way her upward, happy bounce became something of a leap backward as she seemed to realize Katrina stood beside them, watching silently.

"Oh." Felicia bounced backward a couple more times. "That – that should be nice." She bounced a couple steps to the left, putting Luis in between her and Katrina. "So, let's go then, okay?"

Amelia hooked her arm in Katrina's and led the way outside. "Are we stopping for ice cream first?" She really hoped not. She wasn't sure she was up for crazy-flavored ice cream again.

"Let's go straight to the bowling alley," Felicia said. "I'm ready for some fun."

"But I'm starving," Sam said.

"Completely," Luis agreed.

"Yeah, I could really go for a plate of veggies," Mason said.

Amelia rolled her eyes. She had no idea where they put all the food they consumed. Mason and Sam had each eaten their way through two trays of veggies at lunch that day and Felicia hadn't been that far behind them. Luis had actually eaten three full trays of veggies.

Felicia sighed. "Fine. We'll stop at the grocery store on the way and get a bunch of snacks."

"Yes!" The three boys jumped in the air and slammed their hands together in a round of high fives.

Amelia shook her head and just kept walking.

seventeen

the great acorn hunt

MELVIN AND PAULIE stood in the school courtyard and watched as the bunnies left with Amelia and Katrina.

"That is a very disturbing combination-nation," Paulie muttered.

Melvin laughed. "Well, at least Katrina's not eating the bunnies."

"Yeah and that's a shifter miracle there," Paulie said. "You should have seen them in art-art-art today!"

"Katrina's in your art class?"

"Oh, no-no-no. She's in P.E. I think with Sam and Mason, though I couldn't be sure from the distance. Two bunny-bunnies definitely though."

"And you know this how?"

"Melvin, Paulie!" Jake slid to a stop beside them. "Have you guys seen Katrina?"

Paulie rolled his eyes. "She's off making friends with the bunny-bunnies." He waved a hand toward where Katrina stood at the crosswalk, waiting for the light to change.

Jake's eyes got huge. "Aw, furballs." He took off at a run toward his sister.

"This I gotta-gotta see!" Paulie raced after Jake.

Great. This was the last thing Melvin needed. To be chasing after any group Amelia was part of. What if she saw him? What if she got too close and his antlers made an appearance? There was too much open space around here, nowhere to run and hide quickly. He'd be outed in an instant. Shifters everywhere would be outed.

The light changed up ahead and the bunnies, Amelia in their midst, bounced across the street. Jake arrived in time to snag his sister's arm and prevent her from following them.

Keeping an eye on Amelia, to make sure she didn't change her mind, or look back over her shoulder, Melvin hesitantly moved toward where Jake, Katrina and Paulie were huddled.

"What are you doing?" Jake demanded.

Katrina jerked her arm away and rounded on him. "What's your problem?"

"Why are you hanging with the bunnies? It's dangerous, Katrina."

"We're just going bowling. The human invited me. I kind of like her. Don't ask me why, but I do, and she likes the bunnies. So I'm going and I'll be on my best behavior, I promise."

Jake just stared at her.

Katrina rolled her eyes and turned away. "Hey, Melvin. How's the dewlap hangin'?"

"Not bad, Katrina, not bad at all. You sure you'll be okay?"

"Yeah, I'll be fine. What are you guys up to?"

"We're going on an acorn hunt," Paulie said. "We were hoping you guys could help-help-help us."

"Paulie!"

"What? Katrina's already hanging out with the bunny-bunnies. I didn't put her up to it, up to it, so don't look at me like that! Since she's with them already, she'll be the perfect spy. And while she's making sure they're not stealing my acorn-acorns, Jake can help us get another stash hidden in the woods. Then he can help with the stakeout."

"What are you talking about, Paulie?" Jake asked.

"Katrina! What's the holdup?"

Scat! That was Amelia's voice. Melvin shot a panicked look at Jake, who just grinned and made a calm down gesture with his hands. That's when Melvin realized he couldn't actually see Amelia because Jake and Katrina blocked his view. Hopefully if he couldn't see her, she couldn't see him.

"I'll be there in a minute, Amelia!" Katrina called over her shoulder. "Just letting my brother know where I'll be." Katrina turned back around. "Uh, we'd better hurry this up. She looks like she might come back across the street as soon as the light changes."

"Ah, man, I'm so tired of running from that girl." Melvin glanced back at the school, calculating how long it would take him to make it around the building. Too long. About halfway there and he'd be all antlered up.

"Just pay attention while you're with them, Katrina, okay?" Paulie said quickly. "See if they mention my acorn-acorns. Someone's been stealing them and I'm pretty sure it's the bunny-bunnies."

"Why do you think it's the bunnies?"

"I just know, okay?"

"Don't ask him that. Please. You won't get a good answer and we'll all feel insane by the end of the conversation."

Jake laughed. "You'd better get going, Katrina. Light's gonna change any second and if you're not crossing the street, she will be."

Katrina rolled her eyes. "Catch y'all later."

"You'll do it though, right, Katrina?"

Katrina headed across the street, waving a hand to Paulie as she went.

"What does that mean? Jake, what's that mean? Will she spy for us or what?"

Jake laughed again. "Who knows, Paulie? Katrina will do whatever Katrina wants to do, and all we can do is hope that what she wants to do doesn't involve having a little bunny snack."

"Or a human one," Melvin muttered.

"Aw, really? You had to give me that worry too?" Jake huffed in exasperation.

"Come on, Melvin. You too, Jake. You can help us with our Great Acorn-Acorn Hunt."

Jake raised his eyebrows and looked at Melvin, who shook his head in exasperation. "Don't ask. Just join us if you'd like. It should be interesting, if nothing else."

eighteen

strikes and spares

"SO EXPLAIN HOW this works again."

Amelia sighed.

The great thing about yesterday's game was that Felicia and the guys didn't really care about the rules. They just wanted to know the bare minimum to be able to have some fun.

Katrina though was a whole different breed. She wanted to understand all the rules and the requirements for winning. That was her focus. How to win.

Amelia wasn't certain Katrina even knew how to have fun, but she was pretty sure, if Felicia, Luis, Sam and Mason ever lightened up, they would be the perfect ones to teach her.

Amelia explained the rules one more time, which included how points were added up, the way that a strike and spare worked and even the parts of a bowling lane, which required a quick search on her phone.

She'd explained all of this about four times already. Everyone else had already set up on Lane One and they were having a great time, while Katrina and Amelia stood on Lane Two, discussing the ins and outs of a bowling game.

"Why does she keep doing that?" Katrina asked.

"Doing what?"

"That thing where she tosses the ball three lanes over. That's not in the rules."

Amelia laughed. "She's just having difficulty figuring out how to throw the ball. You know. So that it stays in her lane."

Katrina stared at Felicia as she grabbed her second ball, stepped up to the dots on the floor, bounced to the foul line and launched her ball. "She's bouncing."

"I know. It's just too much a part of her personality, I guess. She bounces all the way up and then again when she throws the ball."

Katrina grunted.

"Are your ready to try now?"

Katrina nodded, picked up her ball and stepped up to the first line of approach dots.

Silence fell as Felicia, Luis, Sam and Mason stopped what they were doing to watch Katrina line up her first shot.

Amelia wasn't exactly a great bowler. She'd only been a couple times in her life before moving to Shifferville. Still, she'd seen some pretty fantastic bowling the couple times she'd been. There were always dedicated bowlers to be found at any alley. What she'd seen in the past didn't even come close to what happened next though.

Katrina flowed down the approach with a grace Amelia'd never seen and poured the ball down the lane with an amazing burst of power.

Amelia watched, mouth agape, as the ball spun down the center of the lane at an incredible speed, crashing into the pins and sending them all flying into the pit at once.

"Wow," Luis whispered.

Dead silence fell for a beat, then Felicia squealed and bounced over to Katrina, throwing her arms around Katrina's shoulders in an unlikely burst of affection and joy. "You did it, Katrina! You knocked them all down!" She bounced back and grinned at Katrina in sincere happiness.

"That was amazing, Katrina," Mason said.

Katrina slowly turned and faced them. "Thanks. That was… fun." She sounded amazed as she said the last word.

"You should maybe play against yourself," Amelia said. "None of us are going to be anywhere near that good." She set up Katrina's board so there were three people playing on it: K, Katrina and Kat. "There! Now you can play against yourself and see if you can beat your own awesomeness."

nineteen

stakeout and bowling

THEY'D BEEN IN the woods for hours now and nothing had happened.

"Paulie, they're not going to come and steal your acorns as long as we're hanging around." Melvin climbed down from the tree he'd been hiding in for the past two hours. He was tired and ready to call it a night. "Besides, if you're right and it's the bunnies, they're all at the bowling alley. Having a lot more fun than we are, I might add."

"He's right, Paulie." Jake leapt down from his spot in the tree next to Melvin's. "You need a new plan."

Paulie crawled out from under his bush. "What then? What-what-what am I supposed to do?"

"How about a wildlife camera?" Jake suggested. "We buy one, set it up out here, then we all go home, get a good night's sleep and tomorrow we come back and check the stash. If someone's taken it, they'll be caught on camera."

"That's a great idea. I love that idea." Melvin was in favor of any idea that got him out of the woods.

"Fine." Paulie sighed. "Let's go."

An hour later, the three of them stood in front of the bowling alley.

Paulie had a bag in hand, with a camera inside it. As they'd left the electronics store, they couldn't help but notice how much activity was going on at the bowling alley.

"I thought it was just the bunnies, Katrina and Amelia who were going bowling," Jake said.

"Isn't that the Grizzlies' truck?" Melvin asked.

"And Laney Siamese's porsche-porsche?"

"Ugh," Jake said. "Do not tell me Laney is inside that bowling alley with Katrina. Someone will surely die, if that's the case."

"Let's go check-check it out." Paulie headed for the bowling alley's door.

"Seriously?" Melvin groaned. "Amelia's in there!"

"I know," Jake said. "But Paulie isn't going to let this go, and honestly, I should check on my sister."

Melvin sighed. "Fine. You guys go join the fun. I'll take the camera and get it set up."

"Are you sure?" Paulie hesitated. "I mean, do you know how it works? What if you need help-help?"

"I'll be fine."

"Just make sure you aim it right at my spot. You remember where it is, right?"

"I remember."

"Because we need to be able to see the bunny-bunnies."

"I know. I'll get it done."

"Awesome-awesome. Thanks, Melvin!" Paulie handed over the bag, then turned and followed Jake into the bowling alley.

Melvin shook his head and headed back toward the woods. Once again, his stupid antlers were keeping him from having a life.

A wall of sound greeted Jake and Paulie, when Jake pulled opened the door to the bowling alley.

Music was blaring and people were everywhere, laughing and talking.

Jake led the way through the throngs of people, following the sound of his sister's voice. There was a lot of noise, but he was still able to distinguish her voice from everything else.

Katrina lit up as soon as she saw him. "Jake! You should come play with me. This game is amazing!"

Jake stopped, stunned at the look on her face. She was actually smiling. Katrina never smiled. "Who are you? And what have you done with my sister?"

Katrina made a face. "Come on!" She grabbed his arm and dragged him over to where the human and bunnies were sitting. "Guys, Jake's here. Oh, and Paulie."

Amelia leapt to her feet. "Hi, Paulie! Is Melvin here too?"

Jeez. The rumors were right. The human really did like Melvin. This spelled disaster for everyone in Shifterville.

"No, sorry-sorry. He, um, he went home."

"Oh. Well, at least you guys came."

"Amelia, can you add Jake to the board?" Katrina asked.

"Sure." Amelia stepped up to a weird keyboard and started typing away. "Have we met?" she asked Jake.

"We're in the same art class," Jake said. He wasn't surprised she hadn't seen him before. He'd done his best to stay away from the human. No sense riling up the predator within.

"He's also Katrina's twin brother," Paulie said.

"Wow. I didn't know you had a brother, Katrina. That must be kind of cool, being twins, I mean." She stepped back. "There you go. Jake's on the board. It's nice to meet you, by the way."

Jake grunted. He wasn't sure he agreed. Humans and tigers really weren't meant for friendship.

Amelia turned and started speaking with Paulie and Jake relaxed. He had no idea why his sister wanted to hang out with the human, but he was pretty sure it had nothing to do with friendship, and everything to do with the taste for prey.

"So have you played before, Paulie?" Amelia asked.

Paulie shook his head. Play a human game that he'd never heard of before? Doubtful.

"Let's get you set up then."

Paulie followed Amelia back to the keyboard, where she started adding his name to the boards. It wasn't until she'd finished that he realized she hadn't added him to Jake and Katrina's game, but instead expected him to play with the bunnies! Those blasted, thievin' bunnies!

Paulie scowled.

"Hi, Paulie!" Felicia bounced over to him. "I'm so glad you came. Where's Melvin?" She glanced around, a worried look on her face.

Did everyone assume that he and Melvin were attached at the hip? "He's not here."

"Oh." She smiled. "That's too bad." Her face said exactly the opposite though.

Paulie felt a true stab of pity for his friend in that moment. It wasn't easy being a porcupine-squirrel, not by a long shot, but being a moose-peacock had to be about a million times worse. "Why are all these people here? I thought it was just you guys bowl-bowling tonight."

"Yeah, well, I guess people heard the bowling alley was open and they started trickling in." She leaned forward and whispered, "I think everyone was just super-curious. You know, about bowling and the human and everything."

Paulie nodded. That made sense. Everyone had been curious about the bowling alley since the minute construction began. Now they had a chance to see it in action, to see how the game really worked. Who wouldn't be curious?

"Yes!"

Paulie spun around and stared. Katrina Tiger was doing a little jig, jumping up and down and cheering for her brother, Jake, who had apparently just knocked down – Paulie leaned forward to see better – all the white things.

"Oh, I'm so glad Jake came," Felicia said. "Poor Katrina hasn't had anyone to challenge her. She's been playing against herself all night, she's so good. I think Luis wanted to play against her, but he was too afraid to ask. Besides, he's nowhere near as good as her and he's our best player so far." She bounced a little higher with each word. "Come on, Paulie." She grabbed his arm. "Time to learn how to bowl!"

twenty

the evidence

MELVIN OPENED THE door the next morning to find Paulie and Jake on his front porch, Paulie's hand raised to knock again.

"Finally-finally," Paulie said, pushing his way past Melvin.

"What's up?" Melvin turned and followed Paulie into the house, Jake behind them both.

"I got the camera and I was right-right-right!" Paulie turned, waving it high. "I have all the evidence I need right here. Those thievin' bunny-bunnies are going down."

Melvin rolled his eyes. "All right, let's see it."

While Paulie worked on removing the back of the camera, Jake stepped closer to Melvin and murmured, "Wait until you see this."

"Why? What do you mean? Please don't tell me Paulie's right and it really was the bunnies. I'll never live this down."

Jake just grinned. "Can't promise you that."

Moose balls.

This was going to be bad.

Melvin's only hope was that Paulie was wrong and Amelia wasn't in on it. She couldn't be, right? Because if the bunnies got her involved in stealing Paulie's acorns, that would have to mean the human knew the truth and surely the bunnies wouldn't go that far. Surely they wouldn't reveal their secret to a human, just to mess with Paulie.

"Got it-got it!" Paulie crowed, setting aside the back of the camera. "Watch this!" He pushed a couple buttons on the inside of the camera, then turned the viewing screen to face Melvin and Jake.

"It's just dark, Paulie."

Paulie huffed. "Just a second." He turned the camera back around and fiddled with it some more. "Just gotta fast forward – there!"

He turned the camera back around and as Melvin watched, a bunny slowly entered across the screen, one hop forward, then another.

Was that – Melvin leaned closer.

It was definitely a bunny, but Melvin didn't recognize him. Sure there were a lot of rabbits living in Shifterville and Melvin probably didn't know all of them by name. Anywhere bunnies lived, there were always an awful lot of them, but there was something about this one.

A second bunny suddenly popped its head up from the ground, then scrambled out of what must have been a hole or underground burrow or something.

The two bunnies hopped around, chased one another, sniffed the area and chased one another some more. There was just something about those two bunnies, the way they moved.

The bunnies stopped chasing each other, sniffed the ground, then started digging.

Right at the spot where Melvin knew Paulie's stash was hidden.

No way.

Paulie couldn't be right. It just couldn't be the bunnies who were stealing his acorns.

This was terrible.

The bunnies stopped digging and started rolling acorns out of Paulie's stash, one by one.

That was an awful lot of work for such small creatures. Why didn't they just shift and gather them up and carry them back to their houses? Melvin glanced up at Jake, who just grinned at him, like he knew something Melvin didn't.

Melvin looked back down at the screen.

The two rabbits were now busy rolling the acorns one by one to the spot the second bunny had emerged from a couple minutes before. Several moments passed with the two of them darting to Paulie's stash for acorn after acorn, then they followed those acorns into their burrow, disappearing for good.

"My stash is completely gone," Paulie announced. "I tried to follow them through the burrow, but my porcupine was too big-big-big to fit. There was no following them back to their home. That's okay, though. We know where the bunny-bunnies live and we have the evidence to convict them!"

"Let me see that again." Melvin grabbed the camera and rewound it and watched as the bunnies slowly pushed acorns one by one, nudging them across the ground with their noses.

Melvin looked up at Jake again.

Jake looked like he was about two seconds away from bursting into laughter.

"Um, Paulie–"

"We've gotta go confront those bunny-bunnies. I want my acorn-acorns back, Melvin!"

"Right, but, um, Paulie–"

"Man, don't ruin it. I haven't had this much fun in forever," Jake said. "Let's go to the bunnies' house. This is going to be awesome."

"Awesome! It's not awesome that those bunny-bunnies keep stealing my acorn-acorns!"

"Of course not, Paulie. I just meant it's awesome you caught them red-pawed."

"That's right. I did. Come on, Melvin! I'm going to make sure they can't mess-mess-mess with me anymore!"

Melvin sighed and stood up. "All right. Let's go." He followed Paulie out the door, Jake at his side. "This is really mean, you know," he murmured to Jake. "We should just tell him the truth."

"You really think he's going to believe you?"

Melvin eyed Paulie, who was quivering in his excitement to get to the bunnies, darting ahead, then waiting impatiently for them to catch up, then darting ahead again. "Probably not."

twenty-one

thievin' bunny-bunnies

THEY COULD HEAR the party from a block away.

"Oh, great," Jake muttered.

"What is it?" Melvin asked.

"I completely forgot the reason I left the house this morning. The bunnies are having another of their family get-togethers. This is gonna be just great."

"Wait a minute. If it's a family get-together, shouldn't you be there?"

"Exactly why I left the house so early this morning. I went to check the camera, which is where I ran into Paulie, but really I left to avoid this. Katrina's going to kill me."

"Why?"

"Melvin, every family get-together's torture. It's like a declawing marathon."

Melvin winced.

"Yeah. And I left Katrina to endure the first part of it on her own. All the cousins hate us and our brothers and sisters torture us, so…"

"I'm sure Luis and Felicia don't hate you."

"Okay, fine. They're scared of us. Is that better? Being the only two tigers in a family of rabbits is literal torture, Melvin."

"Your dad's a tiger."

Jake made a scoffing noise. "My mom neutered my dad a long time ago. He might as well be a rabbit."

"Dude, your dad has like forty offspring. I'm pretty sure he's not neutered."

"Whatever. Might as well be. I swear he doesn't even eat meat anymore."

"What? That's not healthy, Jake. Not for a tiger anyway."

"Tell me about it. I don't know, maybe he has a stash somewhere, but he doesn't help us at all. Just lets Mom run roughshod over the two of us, forcing Katrina and me to act like rabbits, eat like rabbits, treat our brothers and sisters like they're not prey."

"Well. Jake. I mean-"

"I know, I know. The last one I get, but the others. I mean, we need meat, man! I swear every day I go without, it's like my brothers and sisters smell even sweeter. And Katrina? Shit, she's holding on by a thread. I expect her to snap any day now. It's why I was so worried when I saw her with the bunnies and Amelia, especially after what happened in P.E."

"Wait. What happened in P.E.?"

"I'm not exactly sure. I wasn't there. But I heard that Luis and Sam were torturing her."

Melvin couldn't imagine how that was even possible. "Seriously?

How do two rabbits torture a tiger like Katrina?"

"It's not like she can eat them, Melvin, and I'm not kidding when I say they smell like prey."

"Come on, guys!" Paulie shouted. "Keep up!"

"We'll talk more later, okay, Jake? Just don't give up. I'm sure we can think of something that will make things better."

"If you say so. Come on." They ran up to Paulie, who was standing just outside the gate of Luis and Felicia's home.

"Guys, there are like a million rabbits on the other side of this gate," Paulie exclaimed.

Jake grinned. "Yeah. Come on. This should be fun." He pushed past Paulie, opened the gate and walked inside.

"Jake!" As they stepped in behind Jake, about fifteen kids, half in rabbit form, half in human form, attacked Jake. One minute he was standing, the next he was on the ground and rabbits were rolling all over him.

"It's about time you got here."

Melvin took one look at Katrina and had to turn away. It was all he could do not to bust out laughing. Anyone else he would have just laughed at, but he was pretty sure Katrina would kill him if he let even a single snicker escape.

She stood there, a look of pure menace on her face. She had a rabbit sitting on her head and two more sitting on her shoulders. All three seemed content to chew on her hair. She had another three bunnies hanging off her left arm and two rabbits sitting on her shoes, clinging to her jeans. Her right hand was propped against her hip, where a ninth bunny was perched, peeking out from under her arm.

Jake didn't move, just cut his eyes to Katrina and started to laugh.

As the bunnies ran all over him, he just lay there and laughed.

Katrina shook her head, but Melvin couldn't help but notice she did it very carefully, not dislodging a single bunny. "You suck, Jake," she said before turning and carefully marching away.

Melvin was amazed to see that not a single bunny slipped from its perch.

"She sure talks a good game," he said to Jake.

Jake sat up carefully. "What do you mean?"

"Well, look at her. Nine bunnies all over her and she's super careful not to drop a single one, let alone take a nibble."

Jake shook his head. "That's just because of our mom, man. No one wants to get on her bad side. Let me tell you. All mama rabbits are scary."

"Come on, guys!" Paulie said. "Stop playing around. We need to find Felicia and Luis."

"Why them?" Melvin asked. "It's not like they were the bunnies in the video."

"I know they're involved, okay?"

Jake stood slowly, lowering bunnies to the ground as he went. "Yeah, but how do you know, Paulie? I just can't see my cousins having anything to do with stealing."

"I saw Luis juggling acorns the other day. He did it just to torment me!"

"Paulie, come on. There are acorns everywhere this time of year." Melvin didn't know why he was even trying to reason with Paulie. It never seemed to work in the past.

"Doesn't matter," Paulie said stubbornly. "I know those were my acorns. I just know it. Come on. We have to find them."

Maneuvering through a rabbit gathering was quite the endeavor, so Paulie and Melvin let Jake take the lead. They followed him through the hordes of bunnies running and digging, through more bunnies sitting around playing board games like Nests and Burrows and around the hay feeders and picnic tables piled high with every vegetable imaginable. They finally arrived at the back of the gathering where the teens were hanging out.

"There you are!" Paulie pushed past Jake to stand in front of Felicia. "I knew-knew-knew it was you! I knew it all along!"

"Hey, what's going on?" Sam stood up and moved to Felicia's side.

Luis arrived at her other side and Mason came up behind her.

"Oh, great. So you're all gonna gang up, gang up against me, huh?" Paulie glowered.

"Paulie, calm down," Melvin said.

"No, I will not calm down, Melvin. These bunny-bunnies stole my acorn-acorns and I demand they give them back!"

"What are you talking about, Paulie?" Felicia asked. "I don't know anything about your acorns."

"Lies-lies-lies!" Paulie pulled his camera out of his backpack. "I have all the evidence I need right here."

"What evidence?" Luis asked.

This was not going to be good. "I knew we should have told him," Melvin muttered to Jake.

"Shhh. This is gonna be great," Jake whispered.

"What's going on?" Katrina wandered up.

"I see you escaped the horde," Jake said.

"No thanks to you. What's Paulie all riled up about?"

That was a good way to describe it, Melvin thought. Paulie was waving his arms and exclaiming about his evidence, but not actually showing them anything.

"Paulie," Melvin said. "Why don't you show them so that everyone knows what you're talking about."

"They know exactly what I'm talk-talk-talking about!"

"Yes, but maybe if you showed them, they'd stop pretending." Melvin raised his eyebrows at the bunnies, hoping they understood that he didn't really believe they were pretending.

Luis grinned. "Let's see your evidence, Paulie."

So Paulie opened the camera, fiddled with the controls, got it fast-forwarded to the right spot and turned the camera so the screen faced the bunnies.

Katrina wandered over to push her way in between Sam and Mason and stared at the screen.

Melvin watched everyone and knew exactly when they figured it out.

Katrina figured it out first. Her mouth dropped open. Her eyes zoomed to her brother and then to Melvin and then she turned and walked away, shoulders shaking.

Luis figured it out next, a split second before Felicia did. Sam and Mason weren't far behind. They watched the video to the very end though, none of them speaking a word.

"Well-well-well?" Paulie demanded, shaking the camera at them. Were they still going to pretend they knew nothing about the theft? "I was right, wasn't I? You can stop pretending now!" Now was the moment. They were finally going to have to admit that bunnies had stolen his acorns.

Felicia cleared her throat. "Well, it does appear you were right, Paulie. Your acorns were stolen by some bunnies."

"Ha!" Paulie crowed. "I knew it!"

Luis snickered.

"What is so funny-funny about that?" They were all looking at him, like they were going to laugh at any moment! Luis was already laughing. What was wrong with these bunnies that they thought stealing was funny? "Those bunny-bunnies should leave my acorn-acorns alone!"

"Well, that's not very charitable, is it, guys?" Felicia asked.

What did that even mean? Not charitable? Did they expect him to just give his acorns away?

"Not at all." Mason shook his head.

"I thought you were nicer than that, Paulie," Sam said.

They did! They expected him to give away his winter stores! "What are you talk-talk-talking about? I'm nice-nice-nice! Just because I'm not willing to give away my acorn-acorns to some blasted, thievin' bunny-bunnies doesn't mean I'm the mean-mean-mean one. They're the mean ones! They stole my acorn-acorns!"

"Yes, but at least you have a home. You have food in your kitchen, Paulie," Felicia said. "Those poor bunnies have to survive the winter. I can't believe you would be so mean to them." She stomped her foot. "You leave those bunnies alone, Paulie. You hear me? They deserve to eat too!"

Paulie stared at Felicia in silence for a moment. She couldn't possibly be saying what he thought she was. Could she? He turned the camera, rewound it and watched the entire theft again, from start to finish.

This time he noticed things he'd missed before. Like the way the bunnies moved. How they didn't look up. How they never shifted, not even a claw or a finger, not even once. How they disappeared into a bunny burrow and never reappeared.

When the video was done, he raised his head and looked at Melvin. "Those are real bunny-bunnies, aren't they?"

"I think so, buddy."

"That is so quill-quilled up," Paulie huffed. He couldn't believe all this time, the thieves were actual, real, non-shifting bunny-bunnies!

Jake burst out laughing. "Oh, Paulie, if you could see your face."

Felicia giggled. "I'm sorry, Paulie. I just couldn't resist. You were so serious. Those are real bunnies, though, yes, and I think they probably need your acorns more than you do. Don't you agree?"

Paulie glowered. "I suppose. Dammit."

"Aw come on, buddy." Luis slung an arm around Paulie's shoulders. "We've got plenty of food here. I'm sure we can find something to take your mind off those acorns."

The Trouble With Tigers (a.k.a. Katrina's Homicidal Urges)

Shifter High: Season 1, Episode 3

Written By

A.J. CULEY

CONTENTS

"Tigers aren't meant to be vegetarians."
- Jacob Tiger

"Which is why we should be allowed to hunt our brothers and sisters without fear of reprisal. Hunting rabbits is a time-honored sporting event in the tiger world."
-Katrina Tiger

one

shiffer square

FINALLY THE WEEKEND arrived. Normally Amelia spent at least part of her Saturdays working with her dad at his vet clinic, but today she was determined to explore more of their town.

Things had been completely crazy since moving to Shifferville and she was determined to figure out why everyone acted so weird around her.

So instead of heading to the clinic where her dad was working, she walked through the woods to the main road that led into town. Soon enough, the woods gave way to a small neighborhood of houses.

As she walked, she caught glimpses of animals darting into bushes and into yards, but no people. At all.

And was that a hedgehog? Even as she noticed the brown ball of quilly fluff, it raced up someone's porch steps and bolted through the pet door.

Amelia hesitated on the sidewalk, listening, expecting to hear at any moment a high-pitched scream from inside the house.

Nothing.

She wondered if she should ring the bell and warn the inhabitants. Someone was in for a surprise when they found the little hedgie burrowed in their home. Taking note of the numbers above the door (9925), Amelia walked on. She'd ask her dad what he thought and if need be, they'd mount a hedgie rescue later that afternoon.

Turning the corner, Amelia headed down another deserted street. Well, deserted in terms of people. Rabbit, squirrel, trio of chipmunks, whoa – raccoon the size of a bear cub.

Even though it was a beautiful Saturday morning, no one was mowing their lawns, going for walks or riding bikes.

It was like a ghost town.

Darn it. Something *was* going on today and it wasn't an all-you-can-eat buffet special or a sudden desire to see the only movie showing at the one theater in town, no matter what Melvin and Paulie claimed. Whatever was going on had to be awesome because the entire neighborhood was deserted.

Amelia increased the pace of her walk and a few minutes later, was standing at the center of the town's square. Before moving to Shifferville, Amelia had always wondered if the town squares she'd seen in movies actually existed in real life.

Now she knew.

They did.

Shifferville's square came complete with a grassy area and pavilion at its center, with buildings on all sides. Shiffer Café and Shiffer Books formed one side, Shiffer Bank and Shiffer Ice Cream Parlor – Amelia shuddered, remembering the taste of their multi-flavored scoop (i.e., seafood surprise) – another. Shiffer Salon and Shiffer Market made up the third side while Shiffer Hardware and Shiffer Bowling were at the fourth. As usual, Shiffer Bowling, which stretched down a side street for a full block, had its lights out.

Well, the missing townspeople hadn't gone bowling, that was for sure. And the movie theater that stretched down a different side street appeared deserted as well.

Amelia desperately wanted to visit the bookstore, to retreat into its stacks and lose herself in a good book, but that wouldn't teach her about this town or its many mysteries.

Unless she could find a book *about* the town and its history.

Amelia grinned and crossed the street at a diagonal, heading for the bookstore. She had just stepped up onto the sidewalk when the lights inside the bookstore suddenly blinked off, the blinds on the front window snapped shut, and the sign hanging in the door flipped from open to closed.

Amelia's mouth dropped open. "Seriously?" She looked at her watch. It wasn't even noon yet. She walked straight up to the door and stared inside. She could see stacks of books, but no people. Someone had to be there. They'd just closed the shop.

Amelia knocked on the window. "Hello? Is anyone in there? Hello? I just wanted to buy a couple books. Hello?"

No movement inside.

Amelia huffed and turned around, propping her hands on her hips. This town was ridiculous.

She wanted to believe the store hadn't closed because of her, that the owner was in a rush to get to wherever the rest of the town had gone, but a part of her just didn't believe it. A very large part of her thought the store owner had seen her coming and had shut her out. Not anyone else. Just her.

She stood there and contemplated what to do next. Would every other store owner close down if she tried to go inside? And if so, why? Why wouldn't they want her to shop for books or clothes or food?

If she remembered right, the café was just next door.

Reaching up to rub her forehead, Amelia used her hand to cover the movement of her eyes as she glanced to the right. The café door was about twenty feet away. Could she make it?

Dragging in a deep breath, Amelia looked to the left as if she might head that way, then bolted to the right.

She lunged for the café door and shoved it open, causing the bell overhead to ring with a clatter.

One swift glance told her there were several groups of people scattered throughout the room, all of them staring at her.

Amelia straightened her spine and avoiding eye contact, strode to an empty booth in the back. She slid in, back to the wall, and slouched down. She drummed her fingers on the table and tried to calm her racing heart.

Why did this town freak her out so badly?

Now she wished she'd invited Felicia to join her. Except if Felicia was with her, Amelia wouldn't discover anything new. Felicia and Luis and all her friends just laughed or made up excuses whenever she mentioned how weird something was. As much as she enjoyed their company, they were part of the conspiracy and were definitely keeping things from her.

Amelia guessed if she ever wanted to figure things out, she'd have to do it on her own, which frankly, kind of sucked. She scowled and continued drumming her fingers. What could possibly be happening in this town that –

All of a sudden, she realized the room was dead silent. None of the people she'd seen were talking or making any noise at all.

A chill raced down her spine and she drew in a slow breath.

This. Right here. This was why the town freaked her out so badly.

She raised her eyes slowly.

There were only three other customers that she could see, a man and two elderly women. They were seated at a table in the center of the room and they were all swiveled in their seats, staring at her.

There was a waitress behind the counter and probably a cook in the kitchen, but Amelia could have sworn there were a lot more people in the café when she first arrived.

More freakishness to make this town unique.

Amelia made eye contact with the waitress. She had the most amazing, brilliant pink hair. "Can I get a menu please?"

"Oh. Um." The woman looked panicked, glancing around. "Um, well, you see."

"We don't have any menus." A huge man stepped out of the kitchen. He was massive. His head brushed the ceilings, which Amelia suddenly realized were awfully high for a cafe. Jeez, how tall was this guy?

The man stepped up behind the waitress, his hand on her shoulder. The woman leaned against him, tilted her head back and smiled up at him. She looked relieved.

No menu. Why wasn't she surprised?

"Okay, um, what do you have that's vegetarian?"

"You don't eat meat?" the woman asked. She looked surprised.

"Not so much, no."

"Really? Why not? Aren't you supposed to be an omnivore?"

"Stella," the big man rumbled.

Stella blanched. "I mean, um, well, isn't it healthier to eat a balanced diet of – um," she glanced wildly at the three customers at the center of the room.

"Vegetables," the man offered.

"And meat," said one of the elderly women.

What was up with these people? Why did they care what she ate? "Probably," Amelia said, "but since my teeth aren't sharp for hunting and ripping apart my prey, I think I'll just stick to my vegetables. Can you bring me a salad or something?"

Stella nodded. "Of course."

The big man disappeared back into the kitchen.

"Do you have Thousand Island dressing?" Amelia asked.

"Um, dressing?"

"You know, to put on the salad."

Stella shook her head.

"You don't have any Thousand Island?"

"We're out," she said, eyes wide.

"Of Thousand Island?"

Stella nodded.

"Okay, how about French?"

"French what?"

"Dressing."

Stella shook her head. "We're out of all the dressings."

"All of them?"

"Uh-huh."

"Okay, fine." What was the deal with this town and salad dressings? "Do you have vinegar and oil?"

"Of course."

"Then I'll just have that."

"On the salad?"

"Yes. On the salad."

"Okay." Stella turned and disappeared into the kitchen, her voice trailing behind her. "Max, she wants vinegar and oil."

"For what?"

"For the salad."

The door swung closed and Amelia couldn't hear Max's reply, but she was pretty convinced it had to be as absurd as the rest of the conversation.

The three other customers were still staring at her.

"Are you really going to put vinegar and oil all over the vegetables?" one of the women asked.

"Jane, leave it alone," the man said.

"Don't tell me what to do, Neil. I want to know if she's going to ruin a perfectly good salad by putting vinegar and oil on it. I was thinking about it and it does seem like the kind of foolishness a hum–humanitarian would do."

"How do you know she's a humanitarian?" the other woman asked.

"She's not eating meat, is she?"

"Wouldn't she be an animalarian then?"

"Don't be ridiculous, Carol. That's not a word and you know it," Jane said.

"It could be a word. You don't know everything."

"Ladies, enough," Neil said. "You'll have the young miss thinking we're crazy."

He didn't need to worry about that. Amelia already *knew* they were crazy, and not just them. She pretty much thought that of everyone in this town. Even the ones she liked, her friends, were kind of crazy. A good kind of crazy, but crazy nonetheless.

Stella settled a giant bowl in front of Amelia with a clatter.

Amelia's eyes widened as she got a good look at her salad. It was the school cafeteria all over again, but at least there, she got to choose what vegetables she wanted. This time, all the madness of the salad bar was in her bowl.

She lifted her fork and slowly sifted through the ingredients. She recognized most of the veggies, but there were quite a few she was certain no one had ever thought to put in a salad before.

Was that cilantro and carrot leaves?

And dear lord, what was that?

There were dark things sprinkled throughout the salad. Maybe they were nuts. She lifted one up. Didn't look like any nut she was familiar with.

"Is that all?"

Amelia jumped, realizing that Stella had been standing at her side this entire time, watching her sift through the salad, waiting for something. "Yes, it looks–um–lovely. Thank you."

Stella grunted and headed back to the counter.

Amelia picked through the strange assortment of veggies and herbs - kale, cilantro, cabbage, parsley, leaves of unknown origin, and was that grass? Surely not. Hesitantly, she nibbled on one of the nut-things.

Salty.

Hard to chew.

And kind of disgusting.

Grabbing her napkin, Amelia wiped her mouth and discreetly spit out the remains of whatever-that-was.

Right. So. Avoid the nuts.

She poked through the salad some more. And found a larger piece of the unknown nut at the bottom of her bowl. She tilted her head. It looked like – surely not.

No one in their right mind would eat an acorn. Would they?

She suddenly remembered a conversation she'd had with Felicia and the gang a while back. They'd seemed surprised at her shelled nuts, almost as if they expected her to eat the shells. She'd laughed and they'd laughed with her, but she'd had a feeling at the time that she was missing something major. Now she had to wonder if they really did eat peanut shells and acorns.

Well, at least she liked kale. Stabbing a leaf, she took a bite and almost gagged.

Holy nibbles and bits!

The leaf was drowning in vinegar. Was there any oil in here at all? She'd never manage to eat this.

Setting down her fork, Amelia picked up the salad and carried it to the counter. "Um, Stella?"

"Yes?"

"I forgot. I'm supposed to help my dad at the clinic. Um, could you maybe box this up for me?"

Five minutes later, Amelia stood on the sidewalk outside the café, contemplating her epic failures that morning. First, she'd failed to explore the bookstore. Then she'd failed to eat at the café. Not that she'd been all that hungry in the first place. She'd just wanted to get a feel for the town, maybe assure herself that it wasn't quite as weird as she believed.

Like she'd said.

Epic. Failure.

Might as well head over to her dad's clinic. Maybe spending time with some animals would cheer her up.

two

fangs & claws

MELVIN MOOSE AND Jacob Tiger glared at each other across the field. They were still in human form, as required by the rules of Fangs & Claws.

Melvin's rack, though, was out and prominent. He'd like to say it was because it was allowed in the game, but while technically true, that wasn't the real reason his antlers were out.

Instead, it was the heady scent of girl everything. Cats, birds, raccoons, bunnies, rhinos, turtles – all the shifter species were at the stadium, either watching or playing, on this gorgeous fall day. With so many females on the field with him and so many others watching from the sidelines, Melvin's inner peacock was strutting proudly, something made more difficult by the fact that Melvin, as a moose, had no tail feathers. Thus, his rack was proudly displayed in their stead.

It was humiliating.

Some of the guys thought it was funny. Paulie, in particular, kept snickering.

Jake, on the other hand, seemed pretty put out.

Melvin figured it was probably because there was someone on the field Jake was interested in, especially since Jake's sister, Katrina, wasn't there. Then again, there were an awful lot of bunny shifters playing. Probably at least some of them were related to Jake, since he had a ridiculous number of bunny siblings and cousins.

Jake let out a roar and raced across the field toward Melvin.

Melvin planted his feet and braced for impact.

Jake was two feet away when a ball sailed between the two of them.

They both swung their attention from each other to it and lunged forward.

There was a huge stampede as every shifter on the field raced for the ball, desperate to be the first to get their claws or fangs (or in Melvin's case, antlers) on it.

Melvin was almost there when Kelly Mole launched herself between him and the ball, catching it with her front incisors. She shifted in mid-air, slammed to the ground and disappeared in one of the many burrows her fellow teammates had dug since the start of the game.

"Not again!" Paulie shouted while the moles and bunnies jumped up and down and cheered.

Melvin just laughed.

"Why is that funny-funny?" Paulie demanded.

"I don't know. It just is. Do you think the shifters who invented Fangs & Claws were burrowing mammals? Because I kind of think they must have been."

A loud clanging sound rang across the field as Kelly popped out of the ground in front of her team's bell, and despite the many shifters waiting for her there, managed to toss the ball right at the bell and score for her team the point that would win the game.

A wave of groans and cheers swelled across the field, as Kelly's team converged on her.

"This suck-sucks," Paulie muttered.

"I think it's pretty cool, actually. I mean, look at Kelly."

Kelly was beaming as her teammates surrounded her, cheering and lifting her from the ground to carry her around the field.

Paulie sighed. "I suppose. This is why we're not supposed to team up by specie-species though."

"The game's over and we lost," Jake snarled, storming toward them. "So maybe you could put that rack away now."

"Hey! It's not his fault-fault."

"It's okay, Paulie. Look, Jake, I would if I could. Seriously. It's the peacock in me. I mean–"

"Well, the peacock in you needs to get it together before the tiger in me decides to take off your head." Jake slashed out with his claws.

Paulie and Melvin leapt back, Jake's claws barely missing them.

"For shift's sake, Jake!" Paulie said. "What's your problem-problem?"

Jake groaned and leaned over, bracing his clawed hands on his knees. "Hacking furballs."

Melvin raised an eyebrow. "You're having furball issues?"

"No, you crazy moose." Jake straightened and flexed his hands, probably trying to make his claws retract. "I'm having meat issues. This herbivore diet is killing me."

"Um, Jake?" Paulie stared across the field. "I don't think you're the only one who's having issues."

Katrina's tiger form walked toward them, a small rabbit dangling from her mouth.

"Fantlers," Melvin gasped. "Isn't that–"

"Son of a shifter. She's got Cory!" Jake broke into a run and raced toward Katrina.

three

shiffer clinic

THE BELL JANGLED as Amelia walked into Shiffer Clinic.

She'd tried to convince her dad to change the name to something more interesting, but he'd refused. He'd said something about tradition and when in Rome, but Amelia thought the conformity of business names didn't reflect tradition so much as a complete lack of creativity.

"Hey, Amelia," Debbie Panda, the receptionist, said.

"Hi." As usual, Amelia found herself trying not to stare at Debbie's hair. She couldn't decide if it was an amazing dye job or just a wig made to resemble a panda's fur. It was pure white, with a black patch over each ear.

"Your dad thought you wouldn't be coming in today."

"Yeah, well, there wasn't much to do in town." Amelia flopped onto one of the chairs in the waiting room. "It was practically deserted. Not a single teenager anywhere."

Debbie nodded. "Yes, they're all probably at –" she stopped

abruptly.

Amelia straightened quickly. "There's a place they usually go on Saturdays?"

"Oh, no." Debbie shook her head. "They're probably just at home. Helping with chores and stuff."

"Debbie, would you call the Foxes? Let them know Timmy's ready to be picked up." Amelia's dad wandered into the room, a baby fox stretched along his forearm, sound asleep.

Amelia gasped and jumped up. "Oh my gosh." She rushed over to her dad.

"Hi, sweetheart. I thought you were off exploring the town."

"Yeah." She stroked a hand down the fox's red fur. "Got bored."

The fox yawned and opened its eyes.

"Hello, baby," Amelia crooned.

"This is Timmy. He had a bit of a stomachache, probably because of the chocolate he ate for dinner last night. Just needed a bit of monitoring."

Amelia suddenly realized her dad looked awfully tired. She hadn't seen him this morning, but that wasn't unusual since he tended to open the clinic early on Saturdays. "Have you been here all night?"

"Pretty much. Timmy's owners were worried, didn't want to leave him here alone so I promised to stay. For some reason, that made them even more anxious. They kept calling all night long. You want to keep Timmy company while I get things ready to close?"

"Sure!" Amelia scooped Timmy into her arms and headed for one of the play rooms. Along the way, Timmy sniffed her sleeve, the collar of her shirt and her chin, his fur tickling her neck and making her giggle.

As she walked down the hall toward the playrooms at the back, Amelia was amazed all over again at the sheer size of her dad's clinic. She loved it there. It was probably the best part of moving to this town. Structured to make all the animals, both big and small, feel safe and at home, the clinic had examination and play rooms of all sizes. There was even a dock off the back of the clinic that led into a huge exam room where her dad could work on the really big animals, like bears and zebras.

That her dad didn't even question these things was what made Amelia crazy. Why couldn't he see how insane all of this really was? One vet in a clinic this size, to work on tiny mice *and* giant bears? It just didn't make sense.

Timmy yipped at Amelia, making her jump.

"Sorry, baby. Let's play a little, okay?" She entered one of the smaller play rooms, settled on the floor, grabbed a ball and tossed it toward the wall.

Timmy leapt out of her arms and tore after it, catching it on the bounce and racing back to Amelia.

She laughed, rubbed his fur and kissed his snout.

Timmy dropped the ball in front of her and she grabbed it and tossed it again.

Thirty minutes later, the Foxes showed up to claim Timmy and Amelia reluctantly handed him over. "He's so sweet," she said.

The woman beamed proudly. "Thank you. He's our first–" She cleared her throat. "Our first adopted fox. We're just so happy to care for him."

After the Foxes left, Amelia's dad said, "Well, Amelia, you want to help me check on the other animals?"

Before she could answer, the door banged open and Katrina Tiger burst into the clinic, her twin brother, Jake, on her heels. Behind them came Paulie and a number of other teenagers Amelia didn't know.

Jake strode forward, a small rabbit in his hands. "He's still breathing, but he won't wake up."

"What happened?" Amelia's dad took the bunny from Jake and stroked a hand down its side.

"A tiger–"

"A tiger!" Amelia exclaimed. "I knew it!" She'd seen a tiger outside the school a couple weeks before, but all her friends had acted like she was crazy. No tigers in Shifferville, they'd insisted, and certainly none roaming free on school grounds.

"A tiger got hold of this bunny?" her dad asked. "And he's still alive?"

"N–no." Jake shook his head and tossed a look at Katrina.

Probably trying to come up with some ridiculous cover story.

"What Jake meant to say was that our dog went for her stuffed tiger, but somehow grabbed the bunny instead," Katrina said. "She dropped Cory immediately. I don't think he's really hurt, just maybe scared."

Yep. Ridiculous.

"Hm." Amelia's dad lifted the bunny's head and peered at its face. "Debbie, would you grab some cilantro from the fridge? We'll be in exam room 3."

"Sure, Dr. Finch."

Amelia followed her dad, Jake and Katrina to the exam room.

As he opened the door, her dad said, "You're lucky your dog didn't bite down. One bite from another animal can be tragic for a fragile bunny."

"We know." Jake glared at Katrina, almost as if he blamed her for what happened. "We're very lucky."

"You should keep the dog away from the bunny," Amelia said, even though she wasn't certain she believed their story.

"She's right," her dad agreed. "Dogs are a real danger to rabbits. And no matter how sweet the dog is, it's still their nature to chase rabbits. You just can't be sure the dog won't hurt him next time."

Katrina looked crestfallen. "I'm sure she didn't meant to hurt the bunny. Is Cory going to be okay?"

Debbie bustled into the room with some cilantro in her hand. "Here you go, Doctor Finch."

"Thanks, Debbie." He held the cilantro in front of Cory's nose, which after a moment, twitched. Amelia's dad brushed the cilantro against the bunny's mouth and Cory's eyes opened.

"See there? Better than smelling salts for humans. Come on, Cory. Stand up now." Amelia's dad lifted the cilantro up a bit so it dangled above the bunny's head.

After a moment, Cory lifted his head and scrambled to his feet. He snatched at the cilantro with his mouth and started chewing.

"Looks like he's going to be fine."

"Thank goodness," Katrina breathed. "My mom would have killed me."

Jake shot her a sharp glance, then reached out and picked up Cory, who was still eating. "Thanks, Dr. Finch."

"No problem at all. Glad everything worked out."

Amelia followed Katrina and Jake back into the lobby.

The teens hanging around jumped up when they appeared.

"He's okay then?" A short girl with long, spiky brown hair asked.

"He's fine, Tessa." Katrina brushed by Jake. "We should get home."

"Wait," Amelia said. "You'll be sure to keep the dog away from Cory from now on, right?" Or the tiger everyone pretended didn't exist.

Yet again, for about the millionth time since moving to town, there was an awkward pause, as if the others in the room weren't certain how to respond to what Amelia said.

Finally, Katrina said, "Yeah, of course. This won't *ever* happen again. Let's go, guys." And she shoved her way outside.

Jake hesitated at the door and glanced back at Amelia. "Tell your dad thanks. And don't mind Katrina. She's just a little upset. She feels responsible since it was her dog that scared Cory. See you at school."

The rest of the teens followed him out the door.

"Hey, Paulie, wait." Amelia caught his arm. "I didn't know there was anything going on today. Where have you guys been?"

"Oh, hey, Amelia-Melia. Good-good-good to see you."

"Yeah, you too. What have you guys been up to?"

"Just um–hang-hanging out."

"But where?" Were they ever going to tell her where they hung out on the weekends? "I went downtown and no one was there."

"Oh. Well. You know. We were play-playing fang-fang-fang-hiking."

"What?"

"Hike-hiking!"

"With a bunny?" She was pretty sure Paulie was lying to her. What had he been about to say? Fang-something.

"No-no-no. Katrina-Rina wasn't with us. She was with her dog at-at-at home and we'd all just gotten back. From our hike. Just in time to see her drop Cory-Cory. The dog, I mean. The dog dropped the bunny-

bunny. So we brought him here."

"Okay. So where's everyone going now?"

"Home. Home-home-home."

Sure they were. "So have you seen Melvin today?"

"Um. Melvin-Elvin? No, no. Not today, no. Why?"

"Just wondering." She couldn't decide if Paulie was telling her the truth or not. Had Melvin been with them, but refused to come inside the clinic because he was avoiding her? Or had he really not been there to begin with?

"Hey, Paulie. You coming or what?" Jake stood in the door of the clinic.

"Yeah-yeah. Coming-coming. Bye, Amelia-Melia."

"Bye, Paulie." Amelia watched them leave, then spun around and shouted, "Hey, Dad, I'm going out!"

"Text me where you'll be," he called back.

"Yep!" She hurried out the door, calling, "Hey, Paulie, wait up!" before skidding to a halt.

There wasn't a single teen in sight, just one lone porcupine waddling into the woods to her left.

"Seriously?" Amelia stalked to the edge of the woods and peered after the porcupine, trying to see where it went. Which was kind of stupid. It was a rodent, which meant it was probably following some trail she couldn't even see or follow as a human.

She let out a huff and set her hands on her hips. She glared at the woods. Did she want to try and explore them? She hadn't even seen where everyone went, which meant she could end up wandering for hours without finding anyone.

Uncertain whether she wanted to go on a wild goose chase through the woods or just give up and convince her dad to rescue a hedgie instead, Amelia paced at the edge of the woods and stewed.

four

survival of the fittest

WHEN JAKE AND Paulie reached the clearing in the woods, they found only Melvin and Katrina waiting for them.

"Where'd everyone go?" Cory had fallen asleep in Jake's arms and he gently pet him as he looked around.

"Back to the arena," Melvin said.

"Hey," Paulie exclaimed. "You're no longer moose-moosified."

It was true, Jake noticed. Melvin's antlers were finally gone, for the first time since they'd arrived at the arena early that morning.

Melvin shuffled his feet. "Um. Yeah."

"But Katrina-Rina's right there!" Paulie waved his arm toward Katrina as if they didn't know who she was. "And she's a girl! Why aren't you all antler-antlered up?"

Melvin shrugged.

"He's right," Jake said slowly. "Now that I think about it, your antlers never come out around Katrina."

"Clawtastic," Katrina muttered. "Like my life isn't screwed up enough, now I'm not even attractive enough for the moose's flirty peacock."

"No," Melvin protested. "That's not it, Katrina. Of course you're attractive."

What exactly did that mean? Jake growled low in his throat and glared at Melvin. Just because they were friends didn't mean the moose was good enough for his sister.

Melvin took a step back. "I-I mean, not that I'm interested," he assured Jake. Then as if he rethinking his answer, he glanced wildly at Katrina and added, "Not that I'm not interested either. It's just–I–I mean–we're all just friends, right?"

Katrina huffed and started pacing again.

Jake knew that meant she'd already checked out of their conversation.

"Wait-wait-wait. So your inner peacock's not trying to impress Katrina-Rina?" Paulie asked.

Melvin shrugged. "I guess not."

"I wonder why. If we can figure it out, maybe you can be around Amelia-Melia without knocking her out again!"

"But I'm not afraid of Amelia!"

Jake barked out a laugh. That was pure Melvin. Poor guy was now turning bright red. Looked like he might flee at any moment.

Katrina stopped her pacing and slowly turned to stare at Melvin, who backed up another step. "What's that supposed to mean?"

"Just that – um – I think my moose… and my peacock… are both kind of scared of your tiger. A little."

Jake could tell by the look on Melvin's face that he was under-exaggerating. By a lot.

"I'm not sure if I should be insulted or complimented," Katrina finally said.

"It's a compliment. Definitely a compliment!" Paulie sighed. "But it's not good, not good news, Melvin. I mean, I'm not sure we can convince your peacock that Amelia-Melia's scary. After all, she's only human."

"Can we stop talking about the moose's issues with his antlers?" Katrina threw her arms up in the air. "We already know it's the Hybrid Effect. It's going to cause problems, probably for the rest of his life, but no one's going to die from Sudden Antler Syndrome." She started to pace again. "Me though. I almost killed Cory! What am I going to do?"

Jake sighed and cuddled Cory a bit closer. "What exactly happened, Katrina? You're usually so careful."

"I know. It's just–I was hunting. I'm so hungry, guys. At least during the week, we get meat at school, but the only way I'm surviving on the weekends is by hunting. I know better than to go after the bunnies, but I lost my head. Their scent is torture. Every day. Hour after hour–"

"Yeah." Jake nodded. It really was torture. Their rabbit siblings smelled delicious. Over the years, Jake had learned to mostly tune out their scent, but Katrina still struggled in a massive way. And their mother insisting on an entirely herbivore diet in the house wasn't helping. At all. "If you were hunting, though, how'd you catch Cory?"

"I don't know! He shouldn't have been in the woods at all." Katrina waved her arms as she paced. "There was a wild rabbit and I thought maybe if I just tasted it, I mean tasted real bunny, maybe the shifter ones wouldn't smell so good, so I chased it. I should have recognized Cory's scent, but there were all these wild bunnies around and I had him in my mouth before I realized who it was. I dropped him immediately, but he just lay there. I thought I'd killed him, Jake."

"I did too." Jake would never forget the sight of Katrina, racing from the woods in her tiger form, their three-year old brother dangling from her mouth. At first he'd thought she was eating him, but then she'd set Cory at his feet and though unconscious, he'd been completely intact, no blood anywhere.

"You probably just scared him," Paulie said. "You know how bunny-bunnies are."

"Yeah, but what if I don't let him go next time? I don't know what I'm going to do."

"Maybe Melvin can help." Jake turned to Melvin, one eyebrow raised. The moose was really smart. He'd helped a couple other shifters learn how to live with the Hybrid Effect. Of course, Katrina's issue wasn't really a result of being a hybrid. If anything, she was too much tiger.

Melvin looked worried, which wasn't a good sign.

"Seriously? Melvin can't even control his own antlers. How's he gonna help me resist my homicidal urges?"

Jake snickered. "Come on. It's not that bad."

"I almost killed our brother!"

"Well, okay, when you put it like that." Jake thought Katrina was being a bit melodramatic, but then again, she'd literally had Cory inside her mouth. If she'd had less control of the tiger– Jake shuddered. He didn't want to think about it.

"You seemed fine at the bunny party last weekend," Melvin said.

"What's changed since then?"

Katrina shook her head. "It's not really a change, so much as just–I don't know."

"An intensification," Jake offered.

"Yeah, that's it. Like most days I'm okay, but some days are harder than others, and lately there have been more bad days than good."

"It's because your tiger's growing stronger," Melvin said.

"How do you know that?"

"My moose senses it. It's happening with all the predators at school. Actually, it's probably true of all of us, but it just seems more intense with the predators. Our shifter sides are maturing with us and for a while, they're going to be harder to control. That's what my mom says anyway."

Melvin's mom was a biology professor at Shifter University, so Jake supposed she probably knew what she was talking about.

"You know what I think, I think?" Paulie spoke up suddenly. "I think maybe it wouldn't be a terrible thing if suddenly there were less bunny-bunnies in the world. Survival of the fit-fittest and all that."

"Paulie!" Jake, Katrina and Melvin all stared at Paulie in horror.

"What-what? What's wrong with that? You know those bunny-bunnies are a nuisance, always stealing my winter stores."

"Now, Paulie, you know the bunny shifters weren't responsible." Melvin rolled his eyes.

Jake grinned at the memory of Paulie ranting over his "proof" that the bunnies had stolen his acorns.

"Well, the wild bunny-bunnies were, so there you go, Katrina-Rina! Anytime you get one of your homicidal urges, feel free to hunt down one of those wild bunny-bunnies."

Katrina made a face. "I can't believe I was hunting them in the first place. It would be like I was snacking on my siblings or cousins. I just need to figure out how to ignore their scent. I don't know how you do it, Jake."

"You think I don't find myself fantasizing about eating one of our brothers or sisters? Especially when they're annoying me?"

"So what are we going to do?"

"I think the first thing we have to do is figure out a way to feed your tigers on the weekends," Melvin said. "So what all do tigers usually eat?"

"Rabbits." Katrina looked hungry.

"Yeah, but what else?"

Katrina looked at Jake.

He shrugged. "Might as well tell him."

"Um." Katrina hesitated.

"Come on. What is it? Can't be more embarrassing than shrubs."

"You know."

"What?"

"Elk."

Melvin blanched.

"And deer. Also, um–"

"Moose?" Melvin looked sick.

"Yeah." Katrina nodded. "Not shifters, of course, but–"

"Okay." Melvin shook his head. "I'm going to pretend I don't know that. Here's the deal though. You can't eat bunny since you're technically half-rabbit. So stock up on a bunch, I mean a ton, of elk and deer jerky, and any other kind that appeals to you – just no rabbit jerky. Keep it at the house and in your pockets at all times, especially when you're around the kids. Just keep sneaking pieces of jerky whenever they start smelling good. It should satisfy your predator and you know, keep the kids safe."

"I don't know," Jake said. "Our parents really don't like us eating meat around the kids."

"You need to tell your parents it's either the jerky or one day, it's you guys snacking on the kids. Trust me. They'll be fine with you eating jerky, especially if you avoid the bunny varieties."

"Do you think that would work?" Katrina asked.

Jake shrugged. "It's worth a try. Let's go pick out some jerky at the store."

"Okay."

"Wait. One other thing." Melvin hesitated.

"What is it?"

"I don't think wild tigers eat meat every day."

"They don't," Katrina said glumly. "They gorge when they do catch meat so they can make it through the lean days."

"So maybe you guys could do that too. You know. Take advantage of the all-you-can-eat school buffet and gorge yourselves at lunch on Fridays."

"We already do that," Katrina said.

"You do?"

Jake laughed. "Yep. It's pretty much the only fresh meat we ever get, so yeah, Katrina and I are completely focused on eating as much as possible at lunch every day."

"I suppose we could try to eat twice as much on Fridays, but I'm not sure I could eat any faster than I already do now."

"Me neither," Jake said.

Melvin looked worried. "Okay, well, hopefully the jerky will work. And if it doesn't, we'll think of something else."

"Yeah, like hunting some bunny-bunnies," Paulie said. "That would be a good alternative, right-right?"

Melvin shook his head. "Just ignore him."

Jake grinned. He couldn't help it. Paulie was such a nut and he really liked him for it. "Yeah, thanks, Melvin. Try not to harass the bunnies too much, Paulie."

"I never harass the bunny-bunnies!" Paulie exclaimed.

Jake laughed. "Come on, sis. Let's go get us some jerky."

As they walked away, Jake heard Paulie say to Melvin, "The bunny-bunnies are the ones harassing me, Melvin-Elvin, not the other way around!"

Melvin's reply, though much fainter, still reached Jake's ears. "I should have told them no moose jerky either. Now my peacock's even more terrified of Katrina!"

five

broken moose

MELVIN BLANCHED. HE shouldn't have said that. What if Katrina heard him? What if she decided to only shop for peacock and moose jerky now?

Paulie snorted. "At least Katrina doesn't steal your acorn-acorns, like those rotten bunny-bunnies."

"You really need to stop blaming the bunnies, Paulie. Haven't you learned your lesson yet?"

"Aw, I was just joke-joking, Melvin."

"Right." Melvin rolled his eyes. "Come on. Let's head back."

A few minutes later, they reached the end of the woods, broke out onto the road in front of the clinic and –

Amelia!

Had she been standing outside the clinic this entire time?

Melvin clapped his hands to his head, shouted, "Gotta go," and hurtled back into the woods. He ran as fast as he could, weaving in and out of trees.

He'd probably run a good mile before he skidded to a stop and bent over, hands on knees.

Staring down at the ground, he gasped for breath and glanced around wildly.

No Amelia.

Thank goodness he got away in time.

As he slowly straightened, he realized his head felt kind of light. *Extremely* light.

And his center of gravity wasn't off.

He reached up and felt the air around his head.

No antlers.

How was that even possible?

He rubbed his head. Not even a tingle.

Thinking back, he tried to remember whether he'd actually felt a tingle when he fled from Amelia or if he'd just panicked and ran without any real evidence of impending antlerhood.

As hard as he tried, he couldn't actually decide whether he'd truly felt that itching pressure or if he'd just imagined it.

Shaking his head, he trotted back to where he'd left Paulie and Amelia, thinking that maybe he'd finally be able to have another conversation with her.

Amelia stopped pacing to stare as Melvin raced away. "Why does he keep doing that?"

"What-what? Doing what-what?"

"Running away!"

"Oh, that, that. Probably just forgot his glasses."

"His glasses were on his face."

"Oh. Don't know, don't know then."

"You have a friend." Was that the same porcupine she'd seen disappearing into the woods earlier? She couldn't tell.

"What-what?" Paulie looked down. "Oh, yeah. Hey there, little guy, little guy." Paulie crouched down and held out his hand to the small porcupine at the side of the road.

"Um, maybe you don't want to get too close."

"Oh, he won't hurt me, will you, buddy-buddy?" Paulie gently stroked the forehead and cheeks of the porcupine.

Was he crazy? Sure porcupines were cute, but – oh. "Is he your pet?"

"Pet? No-no. He's a wild porkie-porkie."

"Why are you petting him then? I don't think that's a good idea!"

Paulie shrugged. "He likes me, likes me. Follows me around anytime I'm in the woods."

"Really?"

"Yep." Paulie fished an acorn from his pocket. "You want an acorn, buddy-buddy?"

The porcupine let out a guttural, squeaking sound – a sound Amelia had heard Paulie make quite a few times – then grabbed the acorn and began to nibble. Had Paulie practiced that sound just so he could bond with his wild friend?

And was Melvin *ever* going to come back?

After a few minutes, Amelia decided the answer was probably no.

With a huff of annoyance, she left Paulie bonding with the porcupine and headed back into the clinic to tell her dad about the hedgehog she'd seen earlier that day.

SH

By the time Melvin made it back to where he'd left Paulie and Amelia, only Paulie was waiting. "Where'd she go?"

Paulie shrugged. "Back inside I guess."

Melvin bolted toward the clinic.

"Hey, Melvin-Elvin. Where're you going?"

Melvin ignored him and shoved open the door to the clinic.

"Melvin Moose!" Debbie Panda stepped out from behind the counter. "What are you doing here?"

Melvin froze. "Uh-"

"Amelia just left, young man! Do you have any idea what would have happened if she'd still been here and your antlers had shown up? If she'd decided to go out the front door instead of the back? You know better than to come to this clinic unless it's an absolute emergency."

"Yeah, but–"

"Well? Is this an emergency?"

"Um, no, sorry." Melvin backed out the door so quickly, he tripped over his own feet and sprawled on the front path leading up to the clinic.

"What's up, Melvin-Elvin?" Paulie stared down at him.

"Nothing," Melvin muttered, scrambling to his feet.

"What was Debbie shout-shouting about?"

Melvin shook his head.

"Go on now! Get out of here before they come back, young man!" Debbie slammed the door shut behind her.

"Yeah, we'd better go," Melvin muttered.

"Where to, Melvin-Elvin?"

“Wherever Amelia went.”

“Wait. You want to see Amelia-Melia? But what about your–” Paulie made a waving motion with his hands to the sides of his head, mimicking a set of antlers. “And where’d they go-go anyway?”

“What?”

“I figured it’d be hours before you were antler-antler-free, but they went away fast this time.”

“Yeah, because they didn’t make an appearance at all.”

“Seriously?”

“Yep.”

“Why not, why not?”

“I don’t know. Maybe because they were out all morning already. Or maybe I just outran my peacock instincts.”

“Or maybe your moose-moose is broken.”

“He’s not broken! I’ve already been moosified twice this morning.”

“Well then, we should test it, test it. See if we can find Amelia-Melia or some of the girls. Not Katrina-Rina though. Let’s go to the arena! Lots of girls will be there.” Paulie started to walk off.

“No, wait. Where do you think Amelia went? She wasn’t inside.”

“I don’t know, do I, do I?”

“It’s just if my antlers aren’t going to come out today, I want to speak with her, get to know her, you know? She won’t be at the arena. Maybe we should try town instead.”

“But if she’s not there, we’ll have wasted our chance when we know there are a bunch, a bunch of girls on the field right now.”

“Don’t care.”

“Aw, come on, Melvin-Elvin.”

“Nope. Town first.” Melvin turned and walked away.

Paulie huffed, then raced after him, grumbling under his breath all the way to town.

six

hunting humans

KATRINA RACED UPSTAIRS to her bedroom, desperate to hide her stash before her mother or siblings scented what she was bringing into the house. She pulled her lockbox out from under the bed, used the key to open it and dumped a bunch of marvelous smelling jerky on top of her journal. The box was full in no time. She locked it, shoved it back under the bed and pulled out a plastic container next. She quickly removed the sweaters and replaced them with jerky. Perfect fit for the rest of her stash.

She leaned over and drew in a deep breath. Such a wondrous, amazing smell. Deer and antelope and elk. Out of respect for Melvin, she hadn't bought moose jerky, even though it had smelled divine.

This jerky stash was a brilliant idea. That Melvin really was a genius.

She went to grab a piece of elk jerky when she scented bunnies.

Lots of bunnies.

Sighing, she replaced the lid and shoved the box under her bed.

And not a minute too soon because suddenly she was covered in her siblings, all of them in rabbit form, of course, which just made them smell all the sweeter.

Swallowing hard, she carefully stood up and began walking slowly to the door, bunnies hopping all around her while others clung to her legs and her arms and her hair. "You guys are crazy," she told them, trying not to smile at their antics.

She'd just reached the hall when she heard the doorbell ring.

A moment later, she heard her mother answer the door and then –

Was that Amelia's voice?

She wandered down the hall and stood at the top of the stairs.

It *was* Amelia.

And her dad.

Had they followed them from the clinic?

But no, Amelia was going on about a hedgehog.

Probably just Tessa.

Jake appeared at Katrina's shoulder. "Is that Amelia?"

"Yeah."

"Who's 'Melia?"

Katrina glanced down and saw that Cory, who had been sitting on her right shoe, was now in his human form, naked.

He jumped up. "Who's 'Melia?"

"The human," Jake said.

Cory grinned and suddenly all the bunnies around them were shifting into their human forms.

"No, no, no, don't go down there," Katrina hissed, but it was too late.

A stampede of naked children raced down the stairs headed for the foyer.

Katrina leapt forward and landed in a crouch on the landing.

That was a mistake. She knew it as soon as she landed.

The leap triggered her hunting instincts and suddenly the scents of bunny and of human were too much. Saliva pooled in her mouth as she imagined scooping up a couple of her siblings and having a morning snack.

Jake caught her from behind just when she might have leapt forward into the living room.

She fought him, but he dragged her back, around the corner.

"Just wait," he hissed.

Katrina's mind was a red haze of hunger, but she still knew she shouldn't eat her brothers and sisters.

The humans though.

They weren't family.

She could make them last too.

She could probably feast on the girl for at least a week.

"Well, thank you so much for stopping by." The sound of their dad's voice caught both their attention.

The humans weren't getting away that easily!

Katrina lunged forward, breaking Jake's grip. Shifting mid-air, she hurtled over the railing, landed in the hall below and raced for the front door.

Amelia was super excited. She couldn't wait to pet the hedgehog. She hoped it was still in the house when they got there.

Her dad had cautioned her that the hedgehog might actually belong to the family in the house, but Amelia couldn't imagine anyone letting their pet hedgie wander the neighborhood. Who had a pet door for a hedgehog anyway?

When they reached the house, Amelia bounded up to the front door. Her dad following at a slower pace.

She rang the doorbell and waited impatiently.

Just as her dad stepped up to stand beside her, the door opened.

"Can I help you?" The woman standing there was short, even shorter than Amelia, and had wavy brown hair with white patches.

Amelia explained about the hedgie and asked if she needed help finding it.

The woman looked confused. "I don't know what you mean. There aren't any hedgies living here. We're a family of –"

"Jana, it must have been when Tessa visited earlier today, remember?" A man appeared at Jana's side. He was a lot taller than his wife, with orange and black striped hair. Amelia stared. His hair was almost identical to Katrina's, though much shorter. "This is Dr. Finch and his daughter, Amelia. "

"Ohhh," Jana said, her eyes widening. "Oh! Well, it's so nice to meet both of you. I'm Jana and this is my husband, Will. And yes, yes, I forgot, Will is quite right. Tessa visited earlier today with her pet hedgie."

"Oh, but the hedgie was outside," Amelia protested. "I thought it was wild."

"Well, yes, yes, it is mostly wild, follows Tessa everywhere, you know."

The words were so similar to what Paulie had said about the porcupine that Amelia stared, uncertain what to think.

"Well, there you go, Amelia." Her dad laughed. "Mystery solved."

Amelia nodded, but she was no longer paying attention to the conversation due to the horde of naked babies that suddenly appeared on the stairs behind Jana and Will.

Seriously.

She tried not to stare, but she honestly couldn't help it.

It was a constant stream of naked babies, giggling and running, their chubby little arms and legs pumping wildly as they chased each other down the stairs, around the entryway and into a room off the hall.

Well, maybe they weren't exactly babies – more like toddlers since they were moving so quickly.

But still!

A horde of naked children!

Will seemed to realize that Amelia's attention had wandered because he glanced over his shoulder, froze for a second, then jerked back around. "Well, thank you so much for stopping by, but we're just fine. Gotta go now." He pulled Jana back and swiftly shut the door in their faces.

"Well, that was rather abrupt," Amelia's dad said as he headed back down the walk toward the car.

Amelia stared at the door, a little stunned at the way their visit had ended.

BAM!

The entire door shuddered from the force of something big hitting it.

Amelia jumped and backed away slowly, the hairs on the nape of her neck standing on end.

The family had seemed fairly – well not normal, with all the naked children running around – but not threatening either, at least not until the end, when Will had slammed the door in their faces.

Now though, all her instincts were screaming that she was in danger.

"Amelia, come on, sweetheart. We can't rescue every animal. It's just not possible."

Amelia backed further down the walk, then turned and hurried to the car. The entire way, she felt as if she had a giant target on her back. She didn't relax until her dad had backed the car down the driveway and turned it toward home.

"That was really weird," Amelia said.

"Weird? How so?"

"Come on, Dad, didn't you see how many kids there were?"

"Kids?"

"Yes! All the children. Don't tell me you didn't notice them."

"No, not really."

"There were tons of kids there, Dad!"

"Well, that's not that unusual. Maybe they run a daycare or one of their kids is having a play date."

"Naked?"

"What?"

"All the kids were naked, Dad!"

"Were they? How very interesting."

Amelia huffed out a breath and rolled her eyes.

This was just so typical.

Her dad was always distracted unless he was dealing with animals. Since the babies running around were all human, her dad hadn't even noticed them. It was like his brain registered and discounted them all at once. If it had been a house full of hedgehogs, though, he would have noted each kind and catalogued any visible injuries in seconds.

Amelia sighed.

Just more proof that her dad would be no help figuring out what was going on in this town.

"Want to get some ice cream before we head back?"

"Sure." Now that she thought about it, the ice cream parlor was the perfect place to get her dad to realize how weird this town was. Seafood ice cream had never sounded so good.

Shifting mid-air, Katrina hurtled over the railing and raced for the front door.

It slammed shut seconds before she reached it.

Unable to stop her forward momentum, she barreled into the door, the force almost knocking her out as she toppled over.

"Just what do you think you're doing?" Her mother stood above her, hands on hips, a furious look on her face. "Were you actually hunting the humans?" A look of horror crossed her mother's face. "You'd better not have been hunting your siblings. You need to stop that right now!"

Jake strode forward. "It's okay, Mom. I'll help Katrina. You might want to – you know – wrangle the bunny-brats."

"I told you to stop calling your siblings that, Jacob Alexander! Do you hear me?"

"Yes, ma'am." He nudged Katrina. "Come on, Kat."

She struggled to her feet and followed Jake through the house to the back door.

"And no hunting the humans!" Their mother shouted after them before slamming the door closed.

A moment later, the door opened again and a pair of jeans and a t-shirt sailed out onto the grass. "And you'd better be shifted in time for dinner, young lady!" The door slammed shut again.

Jake gathered up Katrina's clothes and led her into the woods.

They walked for a while, allowing Katrina to clear her head of the amazing scents of their siblings and the humans.

Eventually, Katrina stepped behind a tree, shifted and got dressed. "Did you remember to put any jerky in your pockets?"

"Naw. You?"

"No, dungit. I barely had time to hide my stash under my bed before the kids were all over me." Katrina would never admit it, but she adored all her bunny siblings. She loved how they would climb all over her and chew on her hair and her shoelaces and the cuffs of her jeans.

She couldn't believe she'd almost eaten Cory. He'd acted normal since waking up, almost like he didn't remember being in the jaws of her tiger. Thank goodness. She wouldn't be able to bear it if her brothers and sisters were scared of her.

Still, things were getting seriously out of hand.

First Cory.

Now the human.

Katrina was beginning to show cannibalistic tendencies, for heaven's sake!

seven

the arena

AMELIA COULDN'T BELIEVE it.

Every flavor in the ice cream parlor was unrecognizable, but her dad didn't even bother to peruse the flavors. Why would he when he knew what he wanted already? He always knew what he wanted.

Vanilla.

And they had it!

Not among the flavors up front, but they had it in the back. And so Amelia's dad had his precious vanilla and didn't even blink when Amelia tried to convince him to try something else. She tossed a bunch of crazy flavors at him - Twigs & Shrubs, Berry Acorn Crunch, Seafood Special, Kale & Spinach – but he just shook his head and said he was happy with vanilla.

Amelia sighed and settled for the same.

"Really?" her dad asked. "You never get vanilla."

"Not when there are normal flavors, no."

"Amelia." He gave her a look that clearly said she was being rude.

Amelia huffed. She wasn't being rude. She was being honest! "Sorry," she muttered. "I just prefer vanilla today."

"All right then. I'm surprised though. Usually you like to try all the unusual flavors."

Amelia made a face. Was he serious?

Surely her dad wasn't that oblivious.

She watched as he happily handed over some money and accepted their two cups of vanilla.

Her turned to smile at her. "Here you go, sweetie."

Yep.

Just when she thought the level of her dad's oblivion couldn't possibly reach any higher, he up and surprised her again.

"I told you we should just go to the arena, Melvin-Elvin!" Paulie paced at Melvin's side, waving his arms in agitation. "We wasted all that time going to town and Amelia-Melia wasn't even there."

"I know, Paulie, but at least we got some ice cream. You really enjoyed the Berry Acorn Crunch."

"True, true, true. I wonder where they got the acorn-acorns though. They better not have stolen my stash!"

"Oh, Paulie, not the stash again."

"I'm just saying!"

"There are acorns everywhere this time of year."

"Yes, and still the bunny-bunnies stole mine instead of getting their own!"

Melvin sighed.

"Let's go this way, this way." Paulie darted into the woods.

"Seriously? Come on, Paulie! You know my moose can't follow those silly porcupine trails!" Melvin glowered into the woods. He couldn't even see where Paulie had gone.

"Hurry up, Melvin-Elvin! Everyone's having fun-fun-fun without us!" Paulie's voice was already growing fainter as he followed some path only he could see.

"Aw, dungit." Melvin shoved his way into the woods, breaking twigs and branches and crushing plants as he lumbered along. "Wait up, Paulie!"

Was that Melvin?

Amelia leaned forward and stared. It *was* him!

He was standing at the side of the road, hands on hips, staring into the trees.

And then he was gone, disappearing into the woods.

"Hey, Dad, stop here, okay?"

"Hmm? What's that, Amelia?"

"I want to walk the rest of the way. Stop here, okay?"

"Are you sure, honey? It's still a bit of a walk to get home."

"Yeah, it's a nice day."

"Okay, just be careful and don't go traipsing through the woods alone."

"I won't." Amelia climbed out of the car and waved as her dad drove off. She waited until he turned the corner, then headed back toward where she'd seen Melvin disappear.

There appeared to be a tiny trail of sorts leading into the woods.

She pulled out her phone, made sure it was fully charged, then stepped onto the trail. Yes, she'd promised her dad she wouldn't go into the woods alone, but she planned on catching up to Melvin, so technically, she wouldn't be alone for long.

She followed the trail of broken branches, moving as quickly as she dared. She was starting to worry that she might have to turn back unless she wanted to risk getting lost when she heard Paulie's voice.

"Hurry up, Melvin-Elvin!"

Amelia grinned and moved faster, hurrying toward the sound of breaking branches and Paulie's fading voice.

She was deep in the woods when she saw it in her peripheral vision.

She didn't even register what she'd seen until a few steps later.

She froze, then slowly backed up to take another look.

Whatever it was she'd seen wasn't there anymore.

Well, part of it was.

There was a raccoon carcass on the ground and it had definitely been partially eaten – gross!

Still, it had to have been her imagination.

Surely she hadn't seen what she thought she'd seen.

Amelia looked around nervously. Whatever had attacked and eaten this raccoon could still be around somewhere.

Whatever it was.

Whatever it was that wasn't what she thought she'd seen.

She backed away slowly.

A faint shout sounded from behind her then several cheers went up.

Amelia swung around and hurried toward the sounds.

Melvin and Paulie arrived at the arena to find a game of Clawball in progress.

There were tons of girls playing on the field and for once, Melvin's antlers didn't make an appearance.

YES!

Now if only Amelia would show up so he could actually talk to her. Though maybe this wasn't the best time, what with all the shifter claws on display at the moment.

"Maybe Katrina-Rina broke your moose."

Melvin scoffed, "How in the world would Katrina Tiger break my moose?"

"Well she was kind of scary, going on and on about how the bunnies smell so good. Maybe your peacock side is in hiding. Forever."

Wouldn't that be nice? Doubtful though. Melvin was pretty sure his antlers were MIA simply because they'd already popped out so many times this morning that he'd lost the ability to shift, at least for a short while. In fact, he figured his antlers would probably come awake any time now. These few moments of glorious freedom never lasted long.

Suddenly Allie Albatross squawked, "I smell the human. She's coming!"

All the animals shifted and scattered, racing into the woods, leaving behind Melvin and Paulie surrounded by a huge amount of torn-up clothes. Before they could decide what to do, Amelia appeared.

"Hey, guys."

"Hey, Amelia." Melvin froze as she moved closer.

Nothing happened. No itching. No tingling. No burning.

That was good, right?

"I thought I heard people talking. Is it just you two out here?"

"Yeah. Just us, just us," Paulie said.

“What’s with all the rags?”

“Don’t know, don’t know.”

“Well, what are you guys doing all the way out here?”

“Well, um, see.” Melvin had no idea what to tell her. Why were they here? To play Clawball. He couldn’t say that!

“We’ve been working to clean-clean-clean the woods,” Paulie exclaimed.

Yes! That was a great idea. “Right. We decided to start here. You know. Clean up all the litter.”

“Well, it’s a good place, I suppose, considering the mess.” Amelia looked around. She leaned over and picked up a shirt. “It’s also kind of… disturbing.”

The shirt had giant claw marks through it.

Amelia raised an eyebrow at Melvin and Paulie.

Melvin shrugged. Our of the corner of his eye, he noticed Paulie doing the same thing.

“Well, come on then. I’ll help.” Amelia started gathering clothes.

Melvin and Paulie rushed to join her.

Soon they had a huge pile of clothing at the center of the arena.

Amelia looked around. “Where’re your bags?”

“Huh?” Melvin asked.

“You know, your bags to put the litter in.”

“Aw, son of a–” Melvin stopped. Shifter. Couldn’t say shifter. He shuddered, realizing he was going to have to watch every word he spoke. No more moosetastic, shiftastic, horned out, dewlapped, furagious… the words he now needed to eliminate were endless!

“So, no bags?” Amelia asked.

“We forgot-forgot them,” Paulie said. “At Jake’s house when Cory got hurt."

Amelia nodded.

Melvin could tell by the look on her face that she didn't really believe Paulie.

For about the millionth time, Melvin wondered what the town council had been thinking when they came up with this ridiculous plan to let two humans move to town. Their secrets were so going to be outed. It was inevitable.

"I can walk you home if you like," Melvin offered.

Amelia smiled. "That'd be great."

Paulie huffed. "I'll just take this stuff to the recycler then. On my own."

"Thanks, Paulie," Melvin said absently as he led Amelia back into the woods.

After Amelia and Melvin left, Paulie sat down to wait. Slowly, bit by bit, shifters came back into the clearing, grabbed their clothes and headed back into the woods to change.

Paulie knew they'd all be going home in rags, but better that than unplanned nudity.

eight

the assembly line

As they walked through the woods, Amelia kept glancing at Melvin out of the corner of her eye. She was frankly amazed he hadn't run away yet. Not that he always ran away, just… most of the time.

"So, how do you like Shifferville?"

"It's okay, I guess. And why does everyone do that anyway?"

"Do what?"

"Say it like that –Shiffffffferville."

"Uh–" Melvin looked stumped. And maybe a little panicked. "I don't know?" He said it like it was a question, rather than a statement.

"It's just weird is all. I mean if it's really pronounced like that, it should be spelled with a few more Fs, don't you think?"

"Yeah, sure, maybe, I guess." He seemed really uncomfortable with the conversation, but then again, Melvin always seemed a little uncomfortable around Amelia.

"What about you?"

Melvin jerked. "Me? What about me?"

"Do you like Shifferville?" Amelia couldn't bring herself to say the town's name like the natives did. It only had two Fs!

"Sure?" Again with the statement sounding like a question. "I mean, it's the only place I've ever lived, but it's good, I guess." He stopped and seemed to think about it for a minute. "No, not good. Great." He sounded more certain, voice strengthening as he continued. "Yes. I do like it here. Yes."

Amelia laughed. "Well, that's good. I guess. What makes it so great?"

Silence. Melvin stopped walking, so Amelia stopped too.

The sun was sinking and the shadows in the woods were lengthening. She glanced around, a bit nervously, realizing how glad she was that Melvin had offered to walk her home. "It's not supposed to be that difficult a question." She laughed. "It's getting dark, so we should keep walking."

"Oh, yes, right."

They started walking again.

Just when Amelia was certain he wasn't ever going to answer her question, Melvin finally burst out, "I like the animals."

Amelia beamed. "Me too! I love animals. It's the best part about this town, I think. I love all the animals in the woods and especially those at the clinic. I even got to pet a baby fox today!"

"Wow. Really?"

"Yes. He was so cute. His name was Timmy!"

"Oh, Timmy Fox."

"Yeah. Timmy the fox." Why had he said it like that? Almost like Timmy was a person. Once again, Amelia found the name thing freaky rather than cool like her dad claimed it was. It was just too weird – every family in town taking the names of the animals they adopted. Before moving to Shifferville, Amelia would never have found it weird to hear someone call a fox by its name, as in Timmy Fox. But now that she'd lived here among people who might be called that, it just freaked her out.

"Right. Sorry. That was kind of weird, huh?" Melvin laughed awkwardly and shuffled his feet. "So what other animals have you seen?"

Amelia's thoughts immediately went to what she'd seen in the woods. "Well, I know this is going to sound really weird, but I swear I saw a rabbit eating a raccoon earlier."

Melvin stopped dead. "A carnivorous bunny?" he asked incredulously. "That had to have been your imagination, Amelia. The woods can be a little spooky at times, but I promise, they don't have bunnies that go around eating other animals."

He sounded so incredulous that Amelia had to believe him. If nothing else, she now knew that Melvin wasn't part of whatever weird was going on in this town.

Knowing that, she decided to confide in him about the visit to the hedgie house.

Melvin laughed as she described the horde of naked children running down the hall.

She was just getting to the part where Will slammed the door in their faces when Jake and Katrina showed up.

"Perfect timing, guys!" Melvin exclaimed. "Amelia was just telling me about a visit she made today. To a house full of naked babies." He grinned at Jake and Katrina.

Amelia wasn't sure what was so funny. Okay, yes, in retrospect it was kind of funny, but that didn't make it any less strange.

"Sounds a lot like your place, guys," Melvin continued.

"What?" Amelia asked.

"Probably," Katrina muttered. "Those kids are crazy, always running around naked."

"They're little," Jake said. "They just haven't gotten used to –" he stopped.

"Used to what?" Amelia asked.

"Wearing clothes," he said.

Amelia wasn't sure that was what he'd been going to say. After all, who had to get used to wearing clothes? "So is it a daycare?"

"No, just our family," Jake said.

"Cousins?"

"No, brothers and sisters."

"Seriously?" Amelia laughed. "All of them? I swear I counted like twenty-three."

"Twenty-nine," Katrina muttered. "Twenty-nine divine-smelling bu-babies."

Amelia raised an eyebrow. What a weird way to describe them. And twenty-nine! That didn't even seem possible. "Twenty-nine siblings? But that means, your mother had thirty-one kids! She didn't even look old enough to have two, let alone thirty-one! Come on, you're pulling my leg."

"Oh." Jake had a panicked look on his face.

"Yeah, you're right. Some are cousins," Katrina said. "They all live with us though. Their parents all – um – died, terrible car accident, you know – so my parents adopted them. It was all very sad, but happened so long ago, we don't even really think about it anymore. My parents are their parents. So don't bring it up or anything."

"Oh, no, of course not." Amelia thought the story was ridiculous though. Thirty-one kids living together? Before she could stop herself, she blurted out her thoughts. "Isn't that an awful lot of people to be living in one house though? I mean is it even safe? I can't believe social services hasn't gotten involved."

"What's that supposed to mean?" Katrina demanded, lunging forward.

Jake caught her around the waist and pulled her back.

Amelia froze.

Katrina's orange eyes were shining brighter than ever and a completely feral look had overtaken her face. "The kids are all healthy and happy. Are you saying our parents can't take care of them?"

"Of course not, Katrina. I'm so sorry." Amelia shook her head. "Everyone seemed perfectly happy. It's just, I've never known a family to have that many kids to care for." She hesitated, not sure if she should ask what she was thinking. It would probably make Katrina even angrier, but if they needed help… Amelia asked as gently as she could, "Is that why they were all naked? Because you can't afford clothes for them?"

"Of course not," Jake scoffed. "They all just got finished shi-showering."

"They shower?"

"Sure. It's faster that way. My mom just holds them in the shower, and washes them one after the other. Otherwise, she'd get soaking wet and so would the whole bathroom. This way it goes faster. She does the girls. My dad does the boys. It's like an assembly line. An assembly line for showering." He looked and sounded so serious, Amelia couldn't tell if he was joking or not.

"Oh, well, I guess that sounds reasonable. I was just going to offer to help, you know, if you–"

"We're fine." Katrina glowered.

Damn. "O-okay." She had to fix this. It had taken too long to get Katrina to finally accept her friendship. "I'm really sorry. I didn't mean to insult you or your family. Forgive me?"

Katrina shrugged. "Whatever," she muttered.

Amelia hesitated, not sure what else to say. It was also getting darker by the minute. "I should really get home. Before my dad calls out the National Guard."

Jake and Katrina looked confused.

Melvin, on the other hand, was looking a little sick. Or maybe panicked.

"Yeah, um, I just remembered, I'm supposed to help my dad–" He flung up his hands, pressing the palms against his temples in a gesture Amelia already recognized as one that signaled impending flight.

Great.

"Um, Jake." Melvin started to back away rapidly.

"Go on, Melvin. We'll walk Amelia the rest of the way home."

"Thanks, Jake. See you, Katrina. Sorry, Amelia." He didn't even look at her as he swung around and barreled back into the woods, shouting behind him, "See you later!"

"Let's go," Katrina growled. She turned and stalked through the woods.

Amelia hurried to catch up. "So, um, the kids were really cute. I'd love to meet them sometime."

Katrina didn't answer.

Amelia racked her brains for something else to say. Anything. "I was telling Melvin how much I really like all the animals in town. I got to hold a baby fox today! His name was Timmy."

Katrina grunted.

"Also, I ran across a raccoon in the woods. I mean not really a raccoon. I mean, yes, a raccoon, but it was dead. Half-eaten. It was really gross." Amelia shivered, remembering the sight of it. The sight of the bunny crouched over it.

She was about to mention the rabbit, when Katrina suddenly stopped and grabbed Amelia's wrist, jerking her forward and shoving her out of the woods. "You're home. As promised."

Amelia stumbled forward and saw that she was facing the back porch of her house. She swung around, but the path behind her was empty. "Katrina?"

No answer.

"Thank you," Amelia called, certain that Katrina could still hear her, even if she wasn't in sight. "See you at school on Monday!"

No answer.

Amelia let out a huge sigh, then turned and headed across the yard toward the back door.

"You were kind of hard on her, don't you think?" Jake asked from his perch in the tree across from Katrina's.

Katrina shrugged, watching as the human walked toward the house. "She was meddling."

"She's human, Katrina. She doesn't understand our world and she was just trying to help."

"By implying we can't take care of our own family?"

Jake shrugged. "The human world's different from ours. You know that."

"Still. She should mind her own business."

"And if the kids were in trouble? If they were hungry or not being taken care of? Would you want her to mind her own business then? Or would you want her to help?"

Katrina growled in exasperation. Of course she'd want the human to help. That wasn't the point! "Let's just go home." She swung out away from the trunk and dropped to the ground.

Jake landed a few seconds later at her side. "Race you!" He took off at a run, darting through the trees.

"Cheater!" Katrina bolted after him.

nine

the jerky solution

WHEN KATRINA AND Jake arrived home, sweaty from their race (which Katrina had won by less than a centimeter), they were dismayed to discover dinner was a salad.

Again.

Katrina wanted a shower before sitting down to the dinner table. She also desperately wanted to get into her stash of jerky, but they hadn't made it two steps into the house before their mother yelled at them.

"Get to the table right now, you two! You're late for dinner!"

That was how Katrina ended up sitting at the table between Cory and his littermate, Callie. Usually, she tried to arrange things so that she sat between her dad and Jake. Anything to keep from having rabbit in reach right when she was sitting down to dinner.

Being late meant those plans were dead in the woods.

How did their dad stand it?

He sat next to their mom, looking so proud of his family, not even a bit unhappy that he'd been doomed to life as a vegetarian tiger.

Katrina was pretty sure her dad had to have stashes of meat somewhere, but he kept them well-hidden from their mom. And from his children. Even the tiger ones.

As she stabbed a piece of kale with her fork – she was so sick of kale! – Katrina glowered down the table at her dad, who laughed at something her mother was saying. How could he just sit there and eat this rabbit food and not want something else? Something better? Something meatier?

She chomped the kale, shuddering at the taste, the texture, the *everything*.

She glanced away and caught Jake's eye.

He grinned at her and lifted his fork, a giant piece of kale stuck on the tines. He shoveled it into his mouth, making a face like it was the best thing he'd ever tasted, then grabbed his neck and pretended to choke.

Katrina rolled her eyes and stabbed another leafy something with her fork. She ate it too. A hideous something that tasted like sweaty socks. She grabbed her glass of water and guzzled to get rid of the disgusting taste. She picked through the salad some more.

Not again.

Her mother had added craisins to the salad. This was so not cool.

Within an hour, all twenty-nine of her siblings were going to be hyper times a thousand, while craisins did nothing for her but make her want to nap. Of course, all fruits and vegetables tended to have that effect on her.

Katrina stabbed another bit of foliage and raised it toward her mouth. At the last minute, she caught a glimpse of yellow.

And dandelions too?

This was going to be a long night.

She raised an eyebrow at Jake and ate her yellows and greens, trying desperately, as she did every night, to chew her food while bypassing all of her taste buds.

As usual, she failed.

A tug on her shirt caught her attention. She glanced over. "What's up, Callie, my love?"

Mouth full of vegetables, Callie just pointed.

Like every bunny Katrina had ever met, her siblings were super-focused on eating when there were vegetables around. In fact, she and Jake were really the only ones who ever talked at the dinner table. Sometimes her dad would laugh or say something to their mom, but most of the time, it was all about the quiet eating.

"More salad?" Katrina leaned forward and grabbed the salad bowl.

Callie nodded, still chewing.

Katrina leaned toward her and scooped a huge helping onto her plate.

That was her mistake. She should have grabbed the plate and leaned toward the salad bowl. Instead she grabbed the bowl and leaned toward Callie, in the process getting a huge whiff of rabbit and prey.

Saliva pooled in her mouth and she imagined opening her jaws wide, canines sliding free and chomping her little sister's head clean o—

"Katrina Tiger! Are you smelling your sister again? You stop that right now! Go to your room, young lady."

Rolling her eyes, Katrina pushed back from the table and headed upstairs.

By the time she hit the door to her room, she was running. She practically dove under her bed to get at her treats.

A plethora of jerky all just waiting for her.

Jake plopped down beside her.

For them.

Sending him a wide grin, she opened the box and they both grabbed handfuls and began to chew.

ten

the hybrid effect

DETERMINED TO MAKE amends for her disastrous conversation with Katrina the day before, Amelia called Felicia the next morning and explained the entire situation. "Katrina loves bowling, so I thought maybe we could get everyone together and go bowling again. I'll go to Katrina's house and invite her personally, but I don't know where everyone else lives and I don't have their phone numbers."

Felicia gulped. "Are you sure that's a good idea? I have Katrina's number. You could just call her."

Amelia was tempted to take Felicia up on her offer, but that wouldn't be right. She wanted to extend the invitation personally.

When she explained that to Felicia, the only response was, "Okay. It's your cremation."

Amelia laughed.

"So, I'll tell Luis. He can call Mason and Sam."

"And Melvin and Paulie," Amelia insisted.

"Right."

"So, do you want to go with me to Katrina's?"

"Oh. Um. Sure."

"Great!"

An hour later, Amelia and Felicia stood on the sidewalk leading up to the Tigers' house.

"Well, go on," Felicia said.

Amelia nodded. "Coming with me?"

"I'll be right behind you."

Right. Felicia was completely intimidated by Katrina. Of course, so was Amelia sometimes, but she refused to let that stop her. Taking in a deep breath for courage, she walked up and knocked on the door. A moment later, it swung open.

Jake stood there. He didn't seem all that surprised to see Amelia.

"Hi, Jake! I wanted to thank you and Katrina for walking me home last night."

He grunted.

"Also, we're all going to the bowling alley and I was hoping you and Katrina would join us."

He just stared at her.

Crikey, he was just as intimidating as his sister sometimes. "Um, so is Katrina here?"

He grunted again, then looked over his shoulder and shouted, "Katrina! Door!"

A few moments later, Katrina wandered up, an adorable toddler hanging off her hip. "Oh," she said when she saw Amelia. "It's you."

"Yeah, hi." Amelia tried a smile, but Katrina just stared, no smile in sight. "Um, so, Felicia and I–" Amelia threw a wild look over her shoulder, noting that Felicia wasn't even on the porch with her, but was hanging way back on the sidewalk. "We're heading to the bowling alley and we were hoping you and Jake would join us." Amelia didn't miss the way Katrina's eyes lit up when bowling was mentioned before she fell back into her usual unreadable, unapproachable expression.

"Bowling," the little boy hanging on Katrina's hip crowed. "Bowling, 'Rina, bowling!"

"Not now, Seth," Katrina said.

"Bowling!"

Several more kids showed up, leaning against Katrina and Jake's legs, peering up at Amelia.

"Bowling?" a tiny girl asked.

"Bowling!" shouted the crowd of kids as even more kids showed up.

"Wow," Amelia whispered.

Jana pushed her way through the kids, shooing them off, wiping her hands on a dish towel. "What's going on?"

"Bowling!" Seth said.

"Um, I came to invite Jake and Katrina to join us for bowling," Amelia said.

"Bowling!"

Amelia smiled. He really was just too cute. "The kids can come too. I mean, if they want."

Jana stared at Amelia for a long, drawn-out moment, then nodded her head. She turned to Jake and Katrina and ordered, "All right, you two. Round up your siblings. Take them for some fun at the bowling alley."

"But, Mom–" Katrina protested.

Jana stopped her protest with a sharp look. "I'm trusting all of you–" she leaned around Amelia to encompass Felicia in her stare, "–to watch over them and keep them safe."

"Yes, ma'am," Amelia said.

Jana nodded and walked away.

Katrina sighed. "Wait here." She shoved Jake back and slammed the door in Amelia's face.

Amelia huffed. "That's twice now," she told Felicia as she walked toward her.

"Twice what?"

"Twice that door's been slammed in my face. I guess we wait."

Fifteen minutes later, the door opened and a stream of kids – this time all of them thankfully dressed – ran out.

Amelia smiled.

A wave of hopping, leaping and bouncing kids surrounded her, demanding her attention. "'Melia, 'Melia, 'Melia," they chanted.

She didn't know any of their names – except for Seth's – but they all seemed to know hers, which was somehow quite charming. "Hi, guys. Let's get walking, okay?"

As they set off, she couldn't help but notice the kids had surrounded Katrina, Jake and Felicia too. They seemed to move from teen to teen in a constant wave of motion, babbling to each other and to the teens and occasionally begging to be carried.

Eventually, after many stops and starts, the four teens and twenty-nine kids all arrived at the bowling alley.

Katrina followed the kids as they poured into the alley, bouncing and calling to each other in excitement. She had to smile at the open-mouthed stares of Luis, Mason and Sam.

"Seriously?" Luis demanded of Felicia.

She shrugged. "Talk to Jake and Katrina. It's their fault."

Luis sneaked a look at Katrina, then shook his head. "That's okay," he muttered and walked away.

An hour later, Amelia had gotten all the bunnies into bowling shoes, set them up with bowling balls and had organized them into teams. She'd explained the rules, set up their computers and let them loose. The alley now rang with the sounds of cheers and groans, of rolling balls and falling pins.

Katrina had been certain she'd be so busy chasing after her siblings with Jake that the two of them wouldn't get a chance to play at all, but instead, Amelia had taken charge and the bunny-brats were all in a state of organized chaos, allowing Katrina and Jake to set their bowling skills against each other.

"You do know why Mom made us bring the bunny-brats, don't you?" Jake asked as he waited for his ball to return.

Katrina just looked at him.

"Craisins," they said in unison.

As if feeding the bunnies sugared fruit the night before wasn't enough, their mom had allowed them to have more craisins in their breakfast bowls that morning.

Jake grinned, grabbed his ball and began his approach.

"At least they're running off their energy several lanes away," Katrina said. Good thing too. She was feeling a might peckish.

Jake laughed as he released his ball, hurtling it down the edge of the lane so that it crashed into one of the two remaining pins, sending that pin flying across the way to knock the other pin into the pit with it.

"Yes!" Katrina shouted.

Jake shrugged. "Should have gotten them all the first time."

"Hey, guys. Can I join your game?" Mason stood to the side, shuffling his feet nervously.

Katrina raised an eyebrow. Surely the rabbit didn't think he could beat them?

"Sure, if you don't mind losing every game," Jake said with a grin.

"I've been practicing," Mason said, "but I can't get any better without someone to challenge me. I keep beating the other bunnies."

"All right then. Let's see what you've got." Jake waved a hand to the lane.

Mason hesitated. "Is that okay with you, Katrina?"

"What? Sure. Go for it."

Mason grinned and headed for the approach dots. He lined up his shot, moved down the lane and threw a pretty decent ball. It raced down the lane, with less power than Jake's, but still with enough speed and aim to send it crashing into the pins, sending nine of them into the pit.

Katrina nodded. "Pretty good."

Mason grinned. "Thanks!"

"Aren't Melvin and Paulie coming?" Amelia asked when she finally got away from the children to join Felicia and the others.

"I called them," Luis said, "but Melvin had other plans and Paulie was ranting about his – " he stopped, a strange look on his face.

"About what?" Amelia asked.

"Oh, just some homework assignment he's working on."

"Oh. So how are you guys doing?" Amelia glanced at their

scoreboard and noticed that only Felicia, Sam and Luis were playing.

"Good, good, good!" Felicia bounced back from where she'd just bowled two gutter balls in a row. "I love this game!" Bounce-bounce-bounce.

Amelia laughed. Nothing ever seemed to get Felicia down. "So, where'd Mason go?"

"He's playing with Katrina and Jake." Sam pointed down the alley.

Amelia turned and stared.

Jake and Katrina had set themselves up several lanes away and sure enough, Mason had joined them.

"Will they annihilate him?" she asked, a little worried Mason might never recover from the trauma of playing the twins.

"Maybe," Felicia said, "but he's pretty good."

"He's been practicing a lot," Sam said. "Spending time at the alley by himself, just throwing balls down the lane."

Amelia stared. "Really? Why?"

Luis grinned. "He likes Katrina."

"Always has," Felicia agreed. "They used to be inseparable, best friends years ago."

"Wow. What happened?"

Sam shrugged. "She got moody, stopped wanting to hang out."

"Plus, she's kind of intimidating," Felicia said.

"And Jake's over-the-top protective of her," Luis said.

"So, were all of you friends?"

"Well, sure. I mean, we're all related, so we grew up together, you know," Sam said.

"You are?"

"Well, most of us are," Felicia said. "Sam's first cousin to Luis and me. His mom is our mom's sister. And our dad's sister is Jake and Katrina's mom, so we're cousins there too. Mason's related to Sam, but not to the rest of us."

"It's fairly convoluted," Luis said.

"I guess so. But also kind of cool. Having such large, extended families, I mean." Amelia wondered how she'd feel about that – if she'd be happy surrounded by so much family or if she'd feel claustrophobic and smothered.

"What about you, Amelia?" Felicia asked. "Do you have any cousins?"

Amelia shook her head. "Not really. It's just my dad and me. He was an only child and my mom's been gone since I was a baby, so it's really only ever been the two of us. It's okay, though. He's a great dad."

"I think that'd be weird," Luis said.

"Yeah, I can't imagine living with only one other person," Felicia said.

"Must. Be. Nice." Sam enunciated each word carefully. "I mean think about it. No long waits for the restroom."

"No nagging from the little ones to share my treats," Felicia said.

"No demands to take them for walks in the woods," Luis said.

Amelia laughed. "Yeah. I guess there are some advantages to being an only child, though I think I would have liked having someone with me when I went for a walk in the woods yesterday."

"I thought you said Jake and Katrina walked you home," Felicia protested.

"Well, sure, but that was later, after I ran into Paulie and Melvin." Amelia wasn't about to admit she'd been following them. "Before then, though, I had to walk through the woods all by myself, finding raccoon corpses and meeting imaginary carnivorous bunnies." Was it her imagination or did all three of her friends freeze when she said that?

"What are you talking about?" Felicia asked.

"I'm sure it was just my imagination getting the better of me." Amelia laughed even though she didn't think it was all that funny. This town was freaking her out. "I swear I saw a rabbit eating a raccoon in the woods. I know it sounds insane, but that's what I saw. Except the rabbit was gone when I checked again, so I must have just imagined it."

The others just stared at her, mouths agape.

"Right?" She really didn't like the way they were looking at her, almost as if they were considering the possibility.

"Of course," Luis said quickly. "I've never heard of meat-eating rabbits."

He sounded sincere to Amelia. Thank goodness. Even though she was sure there was something weird about this town, she wasn't ready to believe it lived outside the laws of nature and science. "Exactly. Which is why it would have been nice to have an older brother walking me through the woods. To keep my imagination from going nuts." Because the weirdness was clearly getting to her.

"I wouldn't know anything about older brothers, though I do have one who's the same age," Felicia said, rolling her eyes at Luis. "I also have tons of younger siblings and older cousins, so feel free to borrow any of them you'd like."

Amelia laughed. "Thanks, Felicia." She stood. Time to see if she'd been forgiven yet. "I'm going to go check on Katrina."

"Sounds good!" Felicia sounded really chipper at the thought.

As she walked away, Amelia couldn't help but wonder if that was because Felicia wanted to talk to Luis and Sam without Amelia hearing, which was kind of paranoid thinking, considering how happy Felicia always was. It really sucked, knowing that her friends were part of whatever conspiracy was happening in this town.

"Do you think it's possible?" Felicia asked as soon as Amelia was out of hearing range.

"Doubtful," Luis said. "I've never heard of a carnivorous bunny."

Sam hesitantly raised his hand.

Felicia and Luis stared at him incredulously.

"Well, I don't actually *eat* meat," he said defensively, "but sometimes it kind of smells good."

"Seriously?" Felicia asked.

"Gross," Luis said.

"But wait," Felicia said. "Does that mean it *is* possible?"

"Not sure," Sam said. "I mean, there is the Hybrid Effect, which I would imagine is why meat smells yummy sometimes. You know."

"Because of your ferret side," Luis said.

"Exactly. Even so, if I had to guess – if there *is* a carnivorous bunny running around, it's probably related to the Tigers."

The three of them turned and stared down the alley toward the seven lanes that had been taken over by the twenty-nine bunny siblings of Jake and Katrina.

As they watched, four bunnies leapt onto a fifth, taking the kid to the ground and rolling around in a mass of writhing, kicking, hollering rabbit mania.

"True," Luis said. "After all, freaky things are bound to happen when a tiger mates a bunny."

eleven

the nature of shifters

"HAVEN'T SEEN YOU in a while, Katrina," Mason said.

Right. Like they didn't see each other every day in school. "So that wasn't you in P.E. last week, hitching a ride on my tiger?"

Mason grinned. "Yeah, well. Sorry about that. Seemed like a good idea at the time."

"A good idea?" Katrina faced him with her fiercest glare. How could he possibly think that? She'd been in her tiger form! Sure she'd been napping in the sun waiting for her turn on the field, but jumping on a sleeping predator was a good way to get eaten. "You're lucky you and Sam didn't end up my afternoon snack."

To her shock, he just laughed. "You don't fool me, Katrina."

"What are you talking about?"

"I know you're struggling with your tiger, but I also know you. We've been friends for a long time, and I'm not afraid of you *or* your tiger."

She huffed. "You should be."

"Why? Because I'm a rabbit?"

"Yes! Because you're prey and I'm predator. Our natures are too different. When we're shifted, I'm about thirty times your size, not to mention my teeth are as long as your head!"

"But we're not shifted now." Mason took a step forward, so that he was in Katrina's space, making her eyes widen. What was he doing? "I'm just as tall as you in this form."

It was true. Katrina hadn't really noticed before, but Mason must have shot up a lot in the last year, for him to reach her height, although – "Only because of your hair." His red hair stood straight up, giving him at least another inch.

Mason grinned. "If you say so."

She sniffed in dismissal and immediately regretted it. His scent filled her nostrils, waking her tiger, but in a different way than she was used to. Her tiger rolled beneath her skin, stretching, wanting out. She clenched her fists. The tiger couldn't come out now. Not with all the bunnies in this trapped space, with the human just a few lanes over, with Mason crowding her, golden brown eyes staring into hers.

"What's going on here?" Jake shoved Mason back, away from Katrina. He had a drink and a bag of chips in one hand, and his other hand was fully clawed, the tip of each claw resting against Mason's chest.

"Jake, knock it off." Katrina edged Mason back, sliding between him and Jake. "We were just talking. This isn't the time or place." Over his shoulder, she could see Amelia heading their way. "Put those away! Amelia's coming."

Jake glowered at Mason over Katrina's shoulder. "Watch yourself, rabbit." He shook his hand, but the claws remained. With a hiss of exasperation, he set down his drink, ripped over the bag of chips and shoved his clawed hand inside.

Katrina figured he was trying to hide his claws in the bag, but instead, they punched right through it.

Jake growled and jerked his claws back inside, but in the process expanded the small puncture into a huge rip and chips began to rain down on the floor.

Katrina shook her head. "Just go away," she hissed.

Shoving his way past Katrina and Mason, Jake snarled. "You're lucky that human's here, rabbit."

"Hey, guys." Amelia watched as Jake stormed across several unused lanes, heading away from everyone. What was his problem? And did he just glare at her?

"Hi, Amelia," Mason said.

Katrina just glowered after her brother.

"What's wrong with Jake?"

"Oh, he's annoyed because Katrina's winning again."

Amelia glanced up at the scoreboard. "Only by a point. Jeez."

"He's competitive," Mason said.

"I guess so. Are you guys having fun?"

"Sure. I love bowling. Don't you, Katrina?"

"What?" Katrina looked at Mason.

"Bowling. It's fun, isn't it?"

Before Katrina could answer, a stream of kids surged into the lane area, surrounding the three of them. "'Rina, 'Rina, 'Rina. We're hungry, 'Rina!"

Amelia laughed. "Uh, yeah, there are some snacks up on the counter and drinks and things, but I don't think we brought enough for everyone."

Katrina shrugged. "That's okay. We should probably be going anyway."

"Oh, but – I was hoping– "

Katrina just stared at her.

Amelia sighed. "Okay. Fine. I guess I'll see you in school then. Unless – do you need help getting the kids home?"

"Naw, Jake and I'll be fine."

"I'll go with them," Mason said.

Katrina looked at him, but didn't say anything.

"Okay. Well, then, um, have a good night."

"Thanks, Amelia," Mason said.

Katrina just grunted.

Amelia watched as the two of them herded all the kids to the door, collecting Jake along the way, who weirdly was pacing along the far wall of the alley.

When the door closed behind everyone, the silence was deafening. Even the soft voices of Sam, Luis and Felicia couldn't penetrate the emptiness of the alley.

Amelia sighed and turned to head back to her friends when the door banged open behind her.

"Hey, Amelia?"

She swung back around.

A halo of sunlight behind Katrina made her a darkened shadow in the doorway.

"Yeah?"

"Thanks for inviting us. We had – fun."

Amelia grinned. "I'm so glad you guys came. I had a lot of fun too."

But Katrina didn't answer. She was already gone.

Amelia shrugged, feeling pretty good about how things went, all in all, and headed over to where Felicia and the gang were still bowling.

"Hey, did they all leave?" Luis asked when Amelia reached them.

"Yeah, the kids were hungry, so Jake and Katrina took them home. I think Mason went along to help."

"Or to flirt." Sam snickered.

Amelia grinned. "Maybe that too."

"That's not good," Felicia said. "I wanted to warn them."

"Warn them about what?" Amelia asked.

"Oh, um, well–"

"Not really them, just Mason, right, Felicia?" Luis said.

"Yeah. I mean, I'd hate for Jake to go after Mason, you know."

Amelia laughed. "I wouldn't worry about Mason. He seemed to be holding his own."

Sam sat up straighter. "What do you mean by that?"

"Well, from what I could see, Jake kind of got in his face, probably because he was standing so close to Katrina, but then Jake was the one who ended up storming off, so I'm guessing Mason won that round."

Felicia looked at Luis and Sam. All of them had weird looks on their faces.

"What? What am I missing?"

Felicia shook her head. "Nothing really."

"No, come on, what is it?"

"Just if Jake stormed off, it was probably because he was trying to control his temper," Sam said.

"Yeah," Luis agreed. "Jake isn't exactly known for walking away from a fight. Unless he wants to, you know?"

"I hope Mason's okay," Felicia fretted. "I can't believe he went with them, with Jake acting that way!"

"I'm sure he'll be fine," Amelia said.

Luis and Sam agreed, saying all the right things, but Amelia could tell, just from the looks on their faces, that maybe they were worried as well, perhaps even more worried than they were willing to admit.

twelve

carnivorous bunnies

"WHAT'S THE RABBIT doing here?" Jake growled, glaring at Mason.

"Cut it out, Jake. Most of our relatives are rabbits, for heaven's sake. The kids like him and we've been friends forever, so stop acting like a jerk."

Jake growled. He couldn't believe Katrina was coming to the defense of that rabbit. "Fine. Just don't try anything funny, rabbit. I'll be watching."

Katrina and Mason both rolled their eyes, which made the tiger in Jake sit up and roar. It was all he could do to contain him.

As they reached the woods, the kids began to shift.

"No!" Katrina shouted. "No shifting!" She raced forward, but it was too late. Clothes were scattered everywhere and bunny tails were disappearing into the woods at a rapid rate. "Jake, help me!"

Jake was too busy laughing to be of any use though. He was surprised to notice that Mason had the same reaction.

The two of them laughed and laughed, bonding in that moment over the ridiculous image of Katrina racing back and forth, grabbing for rabbit after rabbit, only to come up with shredded clothing and not a single bunny.

It took them hours to round up their siblings.

Hours and hours of tracking them down, without the joy of eating at the end of the hunt. Some of their siblings were hunkered down in bunny burrows, bonding with wild rabbits, while others were found in fields of clover and dandelions, eating voraciously. Some were napping in patches of sunlight while others were chasing each other through the woods.

Katrina was panicked the entire time they were hunting, desperate to find their siblings, terrified they'd be eaten by one of the many predators of the woods.

Jake wasn't so worried himself. He thought the bunnies were smart enough to shift if attacked.

Then again, Cory hadn't.

With that one thought, he stepped up his hunting, suddenly and unexpectedly worried for his prey siblings.

He hated to admit it, but Mason was actually quite helpful in rounding them up. He was able to shift to his bunny form and hunt down the bunnies hiding in burrows and other spaces too small for Jake's tiger to access.

Hours later, they had managed to find and return home twenty-eight of their siblings. Only one was still missing.

Katrina was practically in tears. "What are we going to do, Jake?"

"We'll find him, Katrina." Jake slung an arm around her shoulders.

"Remember, Cory's been out here alone before. He probably has all kinds of hiding spots. We just haven't found them yet."

"He's right, Katrina," Mason said. "I'm going to shift again. See if I can scent Cory better in that form." He walked behind a tree and a couple minutes later, a small, red rabbit hopped out.

Mason was honestly the only red rabbit Katrina had ever met, his existence a bit of a mystery in his family as well. No one knew where the red hair or fur had come from, but there was much speculation about an ancestor's affair with a red fox about three generations back. Katrina smiled, remembering Mason's claim a few years ago that his red hair brought him as close to scandal as a boring rabbit might ever get.

It was a bit of a surprise to realize now that she didn't actually consider Mason boring at all. Especially after he'd helped them find so many of their siblings.

Now, as she watched, Mason sniffed his way around the path they stood on, hesitated a moment, then darted beneath a bush and was gone.

"Do you think we should follow him?" Katrina asked.

"Under that bush, down whatever rabbit trail he's following?" Jake said. "I don't think so."

"This is a nightmare. Maybe we should go back home, get some help, before it gets dark."

"Let's wait and see what Mason finds. If he fails, then yeah. We'll go back."

"Fine." Katrina started pacing. "I hate this. I can't believe they just shifted like that. What were they thinking? Mom would just die if she knew." Katrina was pretty sure none of the bunnies would tell their mother what they had been up to, so their cover story, that they were bringing the bunnies home from bowling as they got tired and hungry, was probably a good one, as long as they found Cory before dinnertime.

Which was starting to look highly unlikely.

Their mother was going to kill them.

Rustling came from the bushes and an instant later, Mason ran across the path and disappeared behind the tree where Katrina knew he'd left his clothes.

A couple minutes later, he stepped out, pulling a tee-shirt over his head. "Well," his voice was a bit muffled under the shirt, "the good news is I found Cory." His head popped out of the shirt and he grinned at Katrina.

"You did? Is he okay?" she asked.

"He's fine."

"So where is he?" Jake asked.

"What's wrong?" Katrina just knew something terrible had happened. Even though Mason said Cory was okay, the look on his face was not convincing at all. Plus Cory wasn't with him. "Why didn't you bring him back with you?"

"Well, honestly, it wasn't exactly safe for me to approach him."

"What?" Jake asked.

"What do you mean, not safe? Aw, worms and fleas! A predator's got him, right? That's okay. We're tigers. We can take any predator in these woods. Even bears if we have to. Is it a bear?"

"It's not a predator," Mason said. "Well, not exactly. Anyway, it's just easier if I show you. You need to be quiet though. Stealthy."

Katrina rolled her eyes. "We're tigers, Mason. Stealthy is what we do. Lead the way."

Mason took them on a very circuitous route. At first Katrina wasn't certain why, but then she realized he was maneuvering them downwind of whatever they approached. It had to be something huge. Dangerous.

Her claws slid out. The hair on the nape of her neck stood straight up. She could feel her eyes going feral, her lips peeling back in a snarl.

What was that scent? Prey.

And the sounds of a predator.

Sounds she recognized.

Sounds of a predator ripping apart its prey.

Not Cory!

She shoved past Mason, claws ready to shred anyone who dared harm her brother.

The tiger beneath her skin raked her insides, raging for release.

The blood lust was so strong, at first she failed to understand what she was seeing.

"Holy hacking furballs!" Jake skidded to a stop beside her, claws out, mouth agape.

They both stared at the scene in the center of the clearing.

Little Cory stood in his rabbit form on top of a fallen deer, front claws and face buried in its side. Snarls and growls came from him as he jerked back, a hunk of meat in his mouth.

His hind legs scratched and dug at the deer as he went for another bite.

"What are we looking at?" Jake asked. "Am I seeing what I think I'm seeing?"

"Venison," Katrina breathed, taking in a deep breath of prey. And just like that she lost control of her tiger. Lunging forward, tiger breaking free, she skidded to a stop in front of the deer her baby brother was taking apart piece by piece.

"Great," Jake muttered. "What am I gonna do now?"

"Not sure," Mason said. "But Felicia just texted me. She says Amelia saw a carnivorous bunny in the woods yesterday. Wants to know if that's even possible."

Jake snorted. "I'd say the answer's yes to that one." He stared at the picture his sister and Cory made, snarling over a downed deer. He wasn't even worried about Katrina hurting Cory, not when there was bigger prey to be had. Besides, it looked like Cory could take care of himself.

"So what's the plan, Jake?"

"I'm thinking it's dinnertime. That's what I'm thinking."

"Yeah. I told my parents I was having dinner at your place. Hope that's okay."

"I'm sure it's fine. But just fair warning – this next step's gonna be a little messy." Jake braced himself and strode forward.

After a bit of snarling over who got to carry the carcass (Jake won), the four of them headed home.

Jake was certain they looked a sight coming out of the woods – him carrying the deer over his shoulders, Mason on one side of him, Katrina in tiger form with Cory in rabbit form on her back on the other. As they walked, Jake was quite aware that both Katrina and Cory had their eyes on the deer the entire time. Unwilling to let it out of their sight.

Jake completely understood because it smelled incredible. Or at least it did to his tiger. Jake, on the other hand, would much prefer it at least lightly seared, with pink on the inside, maybe even a little bloody still.

Several times, he almost set the deer down, just so he could take a bite or ten. What would it matter if they ate in the woods or at the dinner table?

Tonight they were having meat for dinner!

Jake didn't even care what his mother had to say about it. Little Cory had risked his life to wander the woods alone, just so he could get some meat.

The more Jake thought about it, the angrier he got.

"What on earth is this?" Their mother stood on the porch, hands on hips, glaring down at them.

Kids poured out onto the porch to stare.

"Wow!" Missy jumped up and down, trying to see. "Is that a deer? Did your tiger kill the deer, Jake?"

Jake shook his head, staring at his mother. "No. It wasn't me."

"Katrina Tiger! How dare you go hunting for meat in those woods? Your siblings play in those woods! And Jake, you know better than to bring your kills to this house!"

"It wasn't Katrina, Mom," Jake said quietly.

"What?"

Cory jumped down from Katrina's back, slipping into his human form on the way down. He ran around to stand in front of Jake and stared up at him. "My deer, Jake! Mine! I caught it, all by myself. It's mine!"

"I know, Cory." Jake didn't look away from their mom as he answered, so he saw the look of shock on her face, saw the way she staggered back. "We're tigers, mom. You married a tiger. You had thirty-one children with a tiger. Maybe twenty-nine of them are bunny shifters, but they all have some bit of tiger in them. Cory needs to feed his tiger half, just the way Katrina and I do."

"I–I didn't –" She shook her head, a look of complete disorientation on her face.

Jake waited while she came to terms with the reality of having a carnivorous bunny son.

"I didn't realize," she finally said. "I just wanted–" She stepped down from the porch and crossed to where they stood. "I didn't want the kids to grow up afraid of their older brother and sister. I never really thought–"

"I know that, Mom. So does Katrina. But we can't live like this. We just can't."

She nodded. "Well, bring the deer inside. I'm not touching it though. You kids want meat, you'll have to prepare it yourselves." She took in a deep breath. "Maybe your dad can help."

"Of course I can!" Jake's dad rushed down the front stairs. He swept Cory up into his arms, not even bothered by his bloody appearance. "You took down this deer all by yourself, son?"

Cory nodded, turning his head to stare at Jake, still unwilling to take his eyes off the deer.

"That's amazing. I'm so proud of you, my boy." He looked at Jake and Katrina. "All of you." Tears stood in his eyes.

Jake wasn't certain if he was teary because he was so proud or simply because he was relieved the meat ban was finally over.

While Jake and their dad got to work on the deer, Katrina raced upstairs to her room, amazed that her mom didn't yell at her for entering the house in tiger form.

She'd just finished getting dressed when a knock came at the door.

She pulled it open, surprised the kids had knocked this time.

It wasn't them though.

She stepped back and her mom walked in. She shoved right up into Katrina's space and hugged her tight.

Her mom's head only came to Katrina's shoulders, making hugs awkward at best, but Katrina hugged her back anyway. "What's wrong, Mom?"

"I'm just so proud of you." Her mom pulled away. "I've given you such a hard time about hunting your siblings. I've wanted you to change, to be more like a rabbit than the tiger you are. Jake, what he said out there, he was right." She began to pace. "I married a tiger because I fell in love with him. I don't know why I decided he had to change. It just seemed the right thing to do. To keep all my kids safe. It was okay when you guys were younger. I thought we'd only have the two kids and that was okay. You were both tigers. It was great."

"And then–"

Her mom laughed. "And then all those rabbit genes kicked into gear. I don't know why it took so long, but suddenly I had all these bunnies to care for and two predator teens who would normally eat bunnies for breakfast and I just didn't know how to handle it."

"It's okay, Mom."

"I'm so sorry, Katrina."

"Really, it's okay." Katrina slung an arm around her mom's shoulders and led her out the door. "Since Jake and Dad are busy getting the meat ready, maybe we should go work on a salad for dinner, okay?"

"That sounds simply delicious."

A couple hours later, the entire Rabbit-Tiger family, with the addition of Mason, finally sat down to dinner.

As usual, the table had large bowls of vegetables spread across it, but at one end, there now stood a platter of lightly seared deer meat as well. A bit of shuffling took place in the seating arrangements, with their dad now sitting at the opposite end of the table from their mom, since the smell of meat made her nauseous and he wasn't about to lose out on his chance to finally eat meat in the house, at the dinner table.

Soon the dining room was full of the sounds of chewing mouths and crunching vegetables. The most interesting part about it was how many of their siblings asked to try the meat. Most of them sniffed it and shoved it away, but a few actually took a bite and announced that it was delicious. Of course, several others said it was disgusting and spat it out.

In the end, Katrina and Jake's twenty-nine bunny herbivore siblings dwindled to only twenty-five. Callie, Jenna and Becca happily embarked upon an omnivore diet, eating meats and vegetables equally. Cory, on the other hand, embraced his newly carnivorous diet, eating almost entirely from the meat platter, with only the occasional piece of cilantro – "for spice," he proclaimed.

"How are those homicidal urges doing?" Jake leaned over to ask Katrina.

She grinned and stabbed a perfectly delicious slice of deer meat. "Feeding the urges, Jake." She glanced over at Jessie, who was busy chomping veggies on her other side and whose scent Katrina's tiger wasn't even aware of.

Instead, the tiger's focus was divided between the deer meat and Mason, who sat across the way, consuming giant piles of veggies and watching her like she was the prey and not him.

He had a lot to learn yet.

"Just feeding the urges."

Continue reading the Shifter High series at

www.ajculey.com/shifter-high.html

thank you for reading

BUNNY TROUBLE

Please consider leaving a review on your favorite book site.

If you would like to know when future installments
of Shifter High will be released,
please sign up at www.ajculey.com/contact.html

other books by A.J. Culey

FOR CHILDREN:

PICTURE BOOKS

A Fairy's Job

If My Cat Could Fly

Salsa Visits the Zoo

Taco Runs Away

TYRABBISAURUS REX

Tyrabbisaurus Rex

Revenge of the Tiger

Zombie Bunnies

FOR TEENS AND ADULTS:

BENEATH THE WILLOW

Sehmah's Truth

Jennara in Flux

SHIFTER HIGH ANTHOLOGIES

Antler Trouble

Bunny Trouble

Prickly Trouble

about the author

A.J. Culey is a teacher, world traveler and writer. She lives with a number of very bossy cats and can be found at her website www.ajculey.com. She can also be followed on Facebook at www.facebook.com/ajculey.author and on Twitter @ajculey.

T-Rab from *Tyrabbisaurus Rex* is also on Twitter @Tyrabbisaurus and can be found there when he manages to coax the laptop away from A.J.

about the illustrator

Professional cover designer and illustrator to authors and publishers worldwide, Jeanine's extensive 17 year professional background includes children's book illustration and publication, comic book art and publishing, book cover art, console game design and product branding.

She is however wondering where T-Rab took her pencils. And if in fact they still exist (she doubts it).

www.ingramcontent.com/pod-product-compliance
Lightning Source LLC
Chambersburg PA
CBHW070615310726
48982CB00001B/92
* 9 7 8 1 7 3 2 3 2 8 6 7 9 *